# DOCTOR WHO AND THE
# TALONS OF WENG-CHIANG

# DOCTOR WHO
# AND THE TALONS
# OF WENG-CHIANG

Based on the BBC television serial *The Talons of Weng-Chiang* by Robert Holmes by arrangement with the British Broadcasting Corporation

## TERRANCE DICKS

**A TARGET BOOK**

*published by*

the Paperback Division of

**W. H. ALLEN & CO. LTD.**

A Target Book
Published in 1977
by the Paperback Division of W. H. Allen & Co. Ltd.
A Howard & Wyndham Company
44 Hill Street, London W1X 8LB

Second impression 1979

Printed in Great Britain by
Richard Clay (The Chaucer Press) Ltd, Bungay, Suffolk

ISBN 0 426 11973 8

# Contents

# Terror in the Fog

They were having a good night at the Palace. Even though it was only the first performance of the evening the theatre was packed. In the boxes and the front stalls sat the toffs, men immaculate in evening dress, ladies in fine evening gowns, all down in the East End for a night at the Music Hall. The body of the theatre and the Grand Circle above were filled with local people, tradesmen and their wives and families, bank clerks and shop assistants. High above in the top most balcony, known as the 'Gods', the poorer people were crowded on to hard wooden benches. Labourers, dock workers, soldiers and sailors, even some of the half-starved unemployed—they'd all managed to scrape together a few coppers for the big night of the week. They were a tough crowd up in the 'Gods', ready to show their feelings with boos, catcalls and rotten fruit if an act wasn't to their liking. But now, like everyone else in the theatre, they were staring entranced at the gorgeously robed figure on stage, the famous Chinese magician Li H'sen Chang.

It was a tough, savage place, this London of the eighteen-nineties; a place of contrasts. Victoria was on the throne, and the British Empire covered much of the globe. England was powerful and prosperous, and London was the trading capital of the world. There were those in the theatre who shared their country's prosperity, spending gold sovereigns with a free hand, living comfortable lives, with servants to look after them. Yet there were many more who were short of the money to pay for their next meal, or even for a roof over their heads. However, tonight they were united in a common aim, to forget their troubles and have a thoroughly good time.

The audience watched spellbound as Chang ushered a smiling chorus girl into a metal cabinet in the centre of the stage. He closed the door, and slid sword after sword through the slots in the cabinet's sides. He waved his hands, withdrew the swords. There was a bang and a flash, and he threw open the door, to reveal the chorus girl, smiling and unharmed. There was a roar of applause. Chang folded his hands in his sleeves and bowed low, and the curtain came down.

Immediately stage hands rushed on, clearing away the props from Chang's act, setting things up for the first act of the second house. Chang went over to a chair, where Mr Sin sat waiting for him.

Mr Sin was a ventriloquist's dummy. He was larger than most, as big as a child or a dwarf. He wore silk trousers and jacket and a little round cap, and his little face was a wooden parody of Chang's handsome oriental features. The little dummy was one of the most popular features of Chang's act. Most magicians performed in mysterious silence, but for much of the time Chang worked with the dummy on his arm. Throughout the act Mr Sin kept up a running fire of disrespectful comment.

Carrying Mr Sin, Chang was making for his dressing-room when Jago, the manager and proprietor of the theatre, intercepted him in the wings. A stout, red-faced figure resplendent in evening dress with diamond studs, Jago was positively glowing with happiness. 'Mr Chang! Wonderful, sir, wonderful. Words fail me!'

Chang bowed. 'Most unusual,' he said ironically.

'Never, in my thirty years on the halls, have I seen

8

such a dazzling display of lustrous legerdemain, so many feats of superlative, supernatural skill.'

It was Mr Sin who answered the flood of compliments. 'Honorable Master,' he piped eerily. 'You are most kind to bestow praise on miserable, unworthy head of humble Chang.'

Jago grinned appreciatively. 'Dashed clever, the way you work the little fellow. Wires in the sleeves, eh?' He held up a hand, interrupting himself. 'Oh, but I'll not pry, Mr Chang. The secrets of the artiste are sacred to me.'

There was a sudden scuffle by the stage door at the far end of the corridor. Casey, the skinny little Irish door-keeper, was trying to prevent a burly tough-looking character from forcing his way into the theatre. As they watched the man broke free, and he came running up to them. Jago was outraged. Members of the public were never allowed backstage. 'What the deuce? You've no right to burst in here like this. Who are you?'

'Name's Buller, sir. Cab driver. I've no quarrel with you, Mr Jago, it's *him* I want.' He shook a massive fist at Chang. 'My Emma came in here last night, and nobody ain't seen her since. Now I'm asking you, mister, what's happened to her?'

Jago grabbed him by the arm. 'Don't trouble yourself, Mr Chang, the fellow's drunk, or mad! I'll have him ejected.'

Buller wrenched himself free. 'You do and I go straight to the police.'

'It is all right, Mr Jago,' said Chang smoothly. 'Do not trouble yourself. I'm sure we can settle this misunderstanding peacefully. If you will come to my dressing-room, Mr Buller?'

There was something almost hypnotic about Chang's

9

soothing voice, and with surprising meekness, Buller allowed himself to be led away.

Jago shrugged at Casey who'd come up to help. 'Courteous coves, these Chinese. I'd have propelled him on to the pavement with a punt up the posterior!' Casey grinned, and went back to the stage door.

Setting Mr Sin on a stool, Chang turned to face his angry visitor. 'Now then, Mr Buller, this missing lady. She was your wife?'

'That's right. Emma Buller. Don't deny she was here, because I saw her with my own eyes.'

'Many ladies come to the theatre ...'

'Not round the stage door they don't. Look, mister, I was passing in my cab, and I saw her as plain as plain.'

'What makes you think it was me she was calling on?'

'She's been acting queer ever since you put the 'fluence on her last week.'

Chang smiled. 'Ah, now I see. She came up on the stage, for one of my demonstrations of hypnotism?'

'That's right—last week. Levitated her, you did. Had her floating up in the air as stiff as a board. She's not been the same since. Affected her reason, I shouldn't wonder. She's been talking about you ever since. And last night she came back to this theatre.'

'Perhaps. But not to see me.'

'Don't come the innocent,' said Buller furiously. 'She's *disappeared*. Nobody's seen her since she came here. I want to know where she is, or I'm calling the law, clear?'

Chang looked at him impassively. 'We have a saying in my country, Mr Buller. The man who goes too fast may step in bear trap.'

Buller stared at him in baffled anger, then turned to

the door. 'You've had your chance. I'm going straight to the peelers.'

As the door slammed behind him, Chang turned to Mr Sin. A very strange thing happened. Although it was on the other side of the room, the dummy turned its head towards him—and smiled malevolently.


Outside the theatre, thick fog swirled through grimy deserted streets that sloped down towards dockland. Gas lamps flared dimly through the fog, and occasionally there came a burst of laughter from some street-corner pub. There was no one about. These little streets had an evil reputation of late. There was fear in the air, almost as thick as the swirling mist.

In a cobbled alley close by the river there was a wheezing, groaning sound, and a square blue shape materialised out of the fog. It was a London police box, of a type that would not come into use for many years. Out of this anachronism stepped a tall brown-haired girl, and an even taller man. The girl was wearing a kind of tweed knickerbocker suit with matching cap, and she seemed obviously uncomfortable in the thick, bulky garments. 'These clothes are ridiculous. Why must I wear them?'

Her companion, that mysterious traveller in Space and Time known only as 'The Doctor', was dressed for the period too, in checked cape and deerstalker cap. He smiled indulgently at her. It was natural enough that Leela should find Victorian clothes constricting. She had been born on a distant tropical planet, one of a colony of settlers from Earth who had degenerated to a near Stone Age level. Leela had grown up as a warrior of the Sevateem, and she usually dressed, and acted, rather like a female Tarzan.

'Be reasonable, Leela,' said the Doctor soothingly.

11

'You can't walk round Victorian London dressed in skins. Don't want to be conspicuous, do we?' The Doctor turned up the collar of his cape, and adjusted his deerstalker to a jaunty angle.

There came a low, booming roar, and Leela dropped into a fighting crouch, reaching for the knife that no longer hung at her waist. 'A swamp creature. That was its attack cry!'

'On the contrary, that was a boat on the river. Excellent. It means we can't be far away.'

'Far away from where?'

'From where we're going!' said the Doctor provokingly.

Leela gave an unladylike snort. 'You make me wear strange clothes, you bring me to this evil place and you tell me nothing——' she began.

'I'm trying to re-educate you, Leela, to broaden your mind. You want to see how your ancestors from Earth enjoyed themselves, don't you?' Ignoring Leela's shrug of indifference the Doctor continued, 'Of course you do. I'm taking you to the theatre.' A garish poster on a nearby wall caught his eye. 'Here we are.' The poster bore a Chinese face and the words, 'LI H'SEN CHANG. MASTER OF MAGIC AND MESMERISM'. 'Li H'sen Chang, eh? I'd rather hoped it would be Little Tich. Still never mind. Come on, Leela, we'll just be in time for the second house.'

The Doctor strode off into the fog, and Leela followed. For all the Doctor's protestations, she was sure this was more for his enjoyment than her education.

Jago closed his handsome gold watch and returned it to his pocket. Anxiously he surveyed the bustle of backstage activity. The first-house crowd had gone, the second-house audience was filing in, and soon it would be time for curtain-up again. A belated chorus girl scurried by on the way to her dressing-room, and Jago gave her a friendly slap on the rump. 'Prance along there, Della, it's time you had your tail pinned on!' The girl giggled and hurried past. Jago's eyes widened as he saw the skinny figure of Casey staggering along the corridor towards him. Casey was doorman, caretaker and general odd job man. He was reliable enough as a rule, though with a weakness for the bottle. Just now he had eyes like saucers, his straggly grey hair was all on end and his grimy collar wildly askew. Jago stared at him. 'What's the matter with you, Casey, got the oopizootics coming on?'

'Mr Jago, I seen it, I seen it again . . .'

Glancing round worriedly, Jago dragged the little Irishman to a quiet corner. 'Quiet, will you? I've told you before . . .'

Casey was beyond all reason. 'It was horrible, Mr Jago, horrible! A great glowing skull coming at me out of the dark . . .'

Jago clapped a hand over the doorman's mouth. 'Do you want to bankrupt me? Keep your voice down. I'll be threadbare in Carey Street if people get the notion the place is haunted.'

Casey's muffled voice emerged from beneath Jago's palm. 'Nine foot tall it was, chains clanking . . .'

'You've been drinking, Casey!'

'Not a drop, sir, I swear it.'

'Then it's time you started.' Jago produced a silver hip-flask. 'Take a drop of this to steady your nerves.'

Casey swigged gratefully at the brandy. 'I ain't never going down that cellar again, Mr Jago. I was just fixing the trapdoor when this apparition rose out of the ground . . . hideous, it was.'

He took another swig at the flask and Jago snatched it back. 'That's enough. It's just your imagination.'

'Never, Mr Jago. Never.'

'Tell you what, I'll come down there with you to-night, soon as the house is clear, and we'll have a good look round. Probably find it's a stray cat ...'

'It's no cat, sir, it's a horrible phantom. I've *seen* it I tell you.'

'All right, Casey, mum's the word. Get back to your work, it's almost time to ring the bell for curtain-up.'

Casey hurried away, and Jago looked worriedly after him. Several times recently the little man had come to him with these tales of a ghost in the cellar. Jago had put it down to a mixture of gin and imagination, but now he wasn't so sure. Whatever it was, he'd get to the bottom of it when the theatre closed. No phantom was going to disturb the smooth running of *his* theatre.


Collar turned up against the cold, hat pulled down over his eyes, Alf Buller hurried through the empty streets towards the local police station. In his mind he was going over and over his story. Probably they wouldn't believe him at first, but he wouldn't go away until he got satisfaction. An English bobby would know how to deal with that smooth-talking foreigner.

Something dropped from a wall, landing just in front of him. Buller looked down unbelievingly. It was Mr Sin, Chang's evil-looking dummy, and in its hand glinted a long-bladed knife.

Buller stood frozen in terror as the little figure stalked towards him.

# 2

## The Horror in the River

The Doctor and Leela were nearing the end of the long alleyway. Leela looked up at the tall buildings all around them. 'A big village, this. What is the name of the tribe that lives here?'

The Doctor grinned. 'Cockneys,' he said briefly.

A hoarse scream pierced the fog—and suddenly cut off. Leela froze. 'The sound of death!'

'Wait here,' snapped the Doctor, and disappeared into the fog. Ignoring his command, Leela hurried after him.

The Doctor turned the corner and came upon a bizarre and terrifying scene. Four black-clad Chinese were dragging a dead body along the pavement.

'Can I help you?' asked the Doctor politely. The nearest man flew at him, knife in hand, and the Doctor promptly knocked him down. Dropping the body, the other three hurled themselves on the Doctor, and he went down beneath a pile of bodies. Leela sprinted round the corner and hurled herself joyfully into the struggle.

There was a wild and confused mêlée, arms and legs whirling wildly in the tumbled heap of bodies. Somewhere on the bottom of the pile the Doctor was clubbed behind the ear with a blackjack, and fell to the ground semi-conscious. The attackers concentrated their attention on Leela. She fought like a wildcat, wishing desperately that she had ignored the Doctor's ridiculous ban on carrying weapons. But she was considerably outnumbered and soon things were going badly for her. Her arms and legs held fast, she saw the glint of a knife coming nearer and nearer to her throat. Suddenly the shrill blast of a police whistle cut through the fog.

Immediately the gripping hands released her as the Chinese ran off. They snatched up the dead body, which had been left sprawled in the gutter, and carried it away with them.

Leela made a desperate grab at the last attacker to flee but he wriggled free of her grip and dashed away —only to be tripped by the Doctor's outstretched foot. He pitched headlong into the road, and Leela pounced like a great cat, grabbing the man's long pigtail and winding it round his throat.

The Doctor staggered to his feet, and set off after the fleeing Chinese with their grisly burden. Through the fog he saw them turn a nearby corner and disappear into a side street. He hurried after them, turned the corner and stopped in amazement. The long straight street stretched away empty before him. The Chinese and their burden had vanished.

The Doctor stood for a moment, rubbing his chin. He had been only minutes behind the Chinese, so they should still have been in sight. There were no side turnings, no alleyways, and they had been hampered by the weight of a dead body. How could they have disappeared so quickly?

The Doctor moved a few paces forward and paused by a round metal shape in the middle of the road. A man-hole cover. He knelt and touched the rim with a finger. Blood.

Aware of angry voices behind him in the fog, he reluctantly straightened up and went back the way he had come.

The Doctor turned the corner to see two burly oil-skinned and helmetted figures dominating the scene.

The police had arrived. One held the remaining Chinaman in a powerful grip, the other was steadily advancing upon Leela, with the traditional cry of the British bobby in times of crisis. 'Now then, now then, what's going on?'

Leela backed away. 'Touch me and I'll break your arm.'

The policeman smiled tolerantly. 'Come along now, miss, don't be foolish ...'

Well aware that Leela was more than capable of carrying out her threat, the Doctor hurried to intervene. 'Good evening, officer,' he said cheerily.

'Keep back, Doctor,' shouted Leela. 'Blue guards! They may be hostile.'

The Doctor ignored her. 'Can I be of assistance, constable?'

'Do you know this young lady, sir?'

'She's my ward. We were on our way to the theatre when we were attacked by this man—and several others.'

The constable nodded ponderously. 'They'd cleared off by the time we got here. All except for this one— the young lady was strangling him with his own pig-tail.'

'Girlish enthusiasm,' suggested the Doctor hopefully.

'You can call it that if you like, sir. *I* call it making an affray. I must ask you to come down to the station with me.'

Puffing contentedly at his cigar, Jago stood watching in the wings, as Chang moved towards the climax of his act. Mr Sin on his arm, the magician stood beside three gilt chairs lined up across the centre of the stage. Lying across the chairs was the same scantily dressed

17

chorus girl who had survived the Cabinet of Death at the end of the first house. She lay stiff and motionless, her eyes closed.

Chang gestured to the audience. 'Please to see, ladies and gentlemen, my subject is now in a state of deep hypnosis.'

Mr Sin's piping, sceptical voice cut through the spattering of applause. 'She has fallen asleep!'

The crowd roared, and Chang looked down at the dummy on his arm. 'No, Mr Sin! She is not asleep.'

'She sleeps! She has been smoking pipe of poppy!'

Again the crowd laughed, this time at the reference to the habit of opium smoking, undoubtedly widespread among the Chinese population of Limehouse.

'Be quiet,' said Chang sternly. 'I will prove young lady not asleep.' He waved to his assistant Lee, who took away the central chair. The girl's body remained rigid, supported only at head and heels.

There was a gasp of astonishment from the crowd, and more applause, interrupted once again by Mr Sin. 'She is lying on metal bar!'

'She is *not* lying on metal bar!' Chang nodded to Lee, who took away the two remaining chairs, leaving the girl floating in mid-air.

Even this wasn't enough to convince Mr Sin. 'You can't fool me. She is held up by wires!'

'Enough!' roared Chang. He dumped the dummy on to one of the gilt chairs, and drew the ceremonial sword at his waist.

The dummy let out a shrill squeak of fear. 'Don't touch me. Help! Police! Murder!'

Chang swished the sword through the air, above the floating girl. 'You see,' he said triumphantly. 'No wires, Mr Sin!'

Jago looked on appreciatively as the act moved towards its climax. No doubt about it, he was a real wonder, this Li H'sen Chang. He congratulated himself on his shrewdness in booking the Chinese magician.

Jago had first heard of Li H'sen Chang through the theatrical grapevine of fellow theatre managers. Previously unknown in the profession, the magician had appeared from nowhere. Perhaps he really was from China as he claimed. After all he really was Chinese, unlike most Oriental magicians who were usually English enough once the make-up was off.

Whatever his origins, Chang's act was brilliant enough to pack any theatre. He was completely professional, never argued about money and never performed for more than a few weeks at any one theatre. He seemed to prefer the smaller halls on the outskirts of London. Jago knew for a fact that Chang had refused several lucrative offers to appear in the West End.

Perhaps he was perfecting his act, thought Jago, planning to take London by storm when he was ready. Not that the act needed perfecting. Jago had watched it night after night, and still had no idea how much of it was done. Take that dummy for instance—sinister-looking thing. But it was wonderful how Chang used it to give variety to his act, lightning the mysterious effect of his magic with Mr Sin's disrespectful jokes.

'I will now demonstrate art of levitation,' Chang was saying. 'I shall raise most beautiful young lady high above own topknot!'

He raised his hand and the stiff body of the girl rose slowly in the air.

This time the storm of applause was uninterrupted by Mr Sin. Jago glanced at the little dummy, slumped on its chair. His eyes narrowed and he looked again. There was a tiny pool of some dark liquid beneath the chair, and as Jago looked another drop splashed from the dummy's hand. It looked exactly like blood ...

Leela looked round the room disparagingly. If this was the home of the ruler, she didn't think much of it. A small whitewalled chamber, furnished with a desk, chairs and a table, all in plain battered wood. More of the blue guards, and behind the desk an older one with strange markings on his sleeve. He was writing in an enormous book, using a metal pen which he dipped into thick blue fluid in a metal pot.

Sergeant Kyle finished his entry, blotted it and looked up at the strange pair before him. He had seen pretty well everything during his service in London's East End, and it was going to take more than a couple of vagabonds to worry him. Routine was routine, and everything had to be dealt with in the proper order.

He stroked his heavy moustache and addressed the Doctor. 'Now then, sir, a few preliminary details if you please. Name?'

'Just call me the Doctor. The young lady's name is Leela.'

Sergeant Kyle gave him a sceptical look, but made an entry in his ledger. 'Place of residence?'

'We've only just arrived here.'

'Your home address will do for the moment,' said Kyle patiently. He looked hard at the Doctor. 'You do have a permanent address *somewhere*, sir?'

'No, Sergeant. We're travellers.'

'I see. Persons of no fixed abode.'

'Oh, we have an abode all right, but it isn't fixed. It's called the TARDIS.'

Kyle put down his pen. 'I could give you and the young lady a fixed abode, sir. Quite easily.' He glanced meaningfully at the heavy iron door that led to the cells.

The Doctor turned to Leela. 'Flat-footed peeler,' he muttered.

'What was that sir?' asked Kyle sharply.

'Nothing complimentary, Sergeant.'

Kyle sighed wearily, and decided to try again. 'Now look, sir, we've got our hands full here at the moment. I don't know if you know it, but there's quite a few girls gone missing from this area. If you'll just co-operate by answering my questions, we'll get on a lot quicker.'

The Doctor was fast losing patience. 'See here, Sergeant, all this nonsense about who we are and where we come from is completely irrelevant. I came here to lay information about a serious crime . . .'

'We'll come to that in good time, sir . . .'

'We'll come to it *now*. We stumbled across a kid-napping, perhaps even a murder, and my friend here caught one of the criminals for you.'

The captured Chinaman was sitting at the wooden table, guarded by a constable. He was staring straight ahead, apparently oblivious to his surroundings.

Kyle gave the man a puzzled look. 'Well, he isn't saying much, sir. And we've only your word about all this.'

'And mine,' said Leela angrily. 'This man and the others were carrying the body of one who had been stabbed through the heart.'

'Indeed, miss? And how can you be so sure of that?'

'I am a warrior of the Sevateem. I know the different sounds of death.' Leela pointed to the motionless Chinaman. 'Now, put our prisoner to the torture and get the truth from him!'

'Well if that don't take the biscuit,' said Kyle wonderingly. 'This ain't the dark ages, you know, miss. Torture, indeed!'

'Make him talk!'

'He happens to be a Chinee, miss, if you hadn't noticed. We get a lot of 'em round here, Limehouse being so close. So we shouldn't understand him if he *did* talk.'

Sergeant Kyle came out from behind his desk and leaned over the prisoner. 'You jaw-jaw-plenty by'n by eh Johnny?'

The man ignored him.

'You see?' said Sergeant Kyle. 'I've sent for an interpreter. We'll get a statement from him soon.'

'Quite unnecessary,' snapped the Doctor. 'I speak Mandarin, Cantonese and most of the dialects.'

'Very remarkable, Doctor. Still, you being a party to the case, it wouldn't really be proper ...'

From somewhere nearby there came the sound of police whistles. Kyle went to the door and looked out into the fog. 'Came from down by the river, that did. They've probably found another floater ...'


The police constable shone his torch out over the river. Beside him a raggedly-dressed man jumped up and down with impatience. 'I tell you I saw it, Guv. Look, there it is, see?' He pointed to a dark shape bobbing on the water.

The policeman looked over his shoulder. 'Where's that boat-hook, then? Hurry, or we'll have to get a boat.'

A second policeman appeared and thrust a boat-hook into his hand. The constable leaned out over the rushing water and made a desperate lunge, hooking the floating shape.

'You got him, Guv,' shrieked the ragged man. 'Don't forget I spotted him first, I gets the reward.'

But as the policeman drew in his catch, even the

ragged man's greed was silenced. The policeman looked down in horror. He had taken many a corpse from the river, but never one like this. Beside him, the ragged man echoed his thoughts. 'Oh my oath. Never seen anything like that in all my puff!'

United in their horror, they stared down at the body. It was savagely mutilated, torn almost to pieces, by giant fangs ...

# 3

## Death of a Prisoner

Stage make-up removed, dressed in everyday clothing, Li H'sen Chang came into the police station and nodded to Sergeant Kyle.

'You sent for me, Sergeant?'

Kyle bustled forward. 'That's right, sir. Good of you to come so prompt.'

Chang spread his hands. 'Not at all. I am finished at the theatre—and I'm always pleased to be of service to London's wonderful police. What can I do for you?'

'Complaint against one of your fellow countrymen, sir, I'm afraid. Lady and gentleman here swear they saw him, together with others not in custody, carrying what appeared to be a dead body. A European body, as I understand it, sir.'

'Indeed.' Chang stared thoughtfully at the Doctor and Leela, who returned the look with equal interest. 'What happened to the others involved in this strange incident?'

It was Leela who answered. 'They escaped. I caught only this one?'

'*You* caught him?' Chang seemed both incredulous and amused. 'How very remarkable!'

The Doctor was studying Chang's face with absorbed interest. 'Don't I know you from somewhere?'

Chang turned away and said abruptly, 'I think not.'

'I'm sure I've seen you somewhere before . . .'

'I understand that to you European gentlemen, we humble Chinese all look alike.'

The Doctor shook his head. 'It's funny, I could have

sworn ... Mind you, I haven't been in China for at least four hundred years ...'

Chang looked significantly at the Sergeant. 'You are taking this gentleman's statement seriously?'

'We have to look into it, sir. Will you be good enough to question this man for me?'

'Of course.' Chang went over to the table and sat down opposite the prisoner. 'Perhaps you could provide me with pen and paper?'

'Of course, sir.'

Kyle went over to his desk, and Chang moved so that his body screened the prisoner from view. He touched the ornate dragon-seal ring on his finger, and a small black pill dropped from the hidden compartment, rolled across the table and landed before the prisoner's folded hands. The prisoner's eyes widened, then he bowed his head submissively. As Kyle brought pen and paper to the table, the man snatched up the pill and slipped it into his mouth.

'Li H'sen Chang!' said the Doctor suddenly. 'I saw your face on the poster. Master of Magic and Mesmerism, eh? Show us a trick!'

The prisoner gave a sudden choking cry, rose to his feet, then slumped dead across the table.

'Very good,' said the Doctor appreciatively. 'How did you do that?'

'I did nothing,' said Chang in a shocked voice. 'Clearly the man has killed himself.'

The Doctor gave him a thoughtful look and went to examine the body, feeling in vain for any sign of a pulse. 'Concentrated poison of some kind. Could be scorpion venom.' He turned over the dead man's hand, displaying the inside of the forearm. 'Do you know what this is, Sergeant?'

Kyle looked at the scorpion tattoo. 'It's a Tong sign, isn't it, sir?'

'The Tong of the Black Scorpion. Probably one of the most dangerous criminal organisations in the world —wouldn't you agree, Li H'sen Chang?'

Chang rose from the table. 'If it is a Tong sign, Sergeant, your mystery is solved. Many of my misguided countrymen belong to these organisations—they have frequent wars among themselves. I imagine you stumbled upon an incident in such a war. Your prisoner committed suicide, rather than be forced to speak—the other killers and their victim will never be found. A truly regrettable incident, but one that is now closed.' Chang moved towards the door, pausing a moment in front of Leela. 'Perhaps we shall meet again in more pleasant circumstances?' There was an undertone of menace in the remark that made it sound almost like a challenge.

'Perhaps we shall,' said Leela flatly. Chang nodded coolly to the Doctor, and disappeared into the night.

Sergeant Kyle scratched his head, looking at the body of his late prisoner, then back to the Doctor and Leela. 'Blowed if I know what to do about all this, and that's a fact.'

'Then I'll tell you,' said the Doctor crisply. 'You can start by getting this body to the nearest mortuary and arranging for an immediate post mortem. I need to know whether my theory about scorpion venom is correct.'

'*You* need to know, sir?'

'My dear Sergeant, if the Tong of the Black Scorpion is active here in London, you're going to need my help. Now cut along and do as I ask.'

Such was the authority in the Doctor's voice that Kyle found himself obeying without question. 'Constable,' he called. 'Get out the ambulance-cart and wheel this body round to the mortuary. Ask Professor Litefoot to perform an immediate post mortem.'

In the Palace Theatre all was dark and still. The audience had gone, the performers and stage staff had gone, and Casey the caretaker was alone backstage—alone, that is, except for Jago who appeared suddenly in the backstage corridor and said reproachfully, 'Twinkle, twinkle out in front, Casey. The gallery lights are still burning.'

'Just going to see to them, Mr Jago.'

'Everyone else gone?'

'That they have, Mr Jago. I've just locked the stage door.'

'I hope those girls have the sense to go straight home to their digs.'

'That they will, sir, with all these disappearances in the papers.' He lowered his voice to a ghoulish whisper. 'There's nine of 'em now, sir. Nine girls missing, vanished off the streets—and all in this area too.'

Jago shrugged. 'They were probably stony broke. Scarpered because they couldn't pay the rent. You cut along and turn those gallery lights out. I'll wait for you here.'

Casey headed for the stairs and Jago paused for a moment, lost in thought. Slowly, almost unwillingly, he began walking towards Chang's dressing-room.

He opened the door cautiously and looked inside. Everything was quiet. He went to the wicker hamper that lay beside Chang's make-up and opened the lid. Mr Sin lay staring lifelessly up at him.

Jago reached into the basket and lifted the wooden hand—and the dummy's eyes flew open. Letting go the hand, Jago jumped back in alarm. Then he grinned ruefully. Moving the arm must have operated the eye mechanism. He gave the dummy a cautious shake and the eyes clicked shut.

He lifted the arm again, and rubbed the wooden hand with his handkerchief. There was a faint red stain on the white silk. 'It *was* blood,' muttered Jago. 'Blood all over the hand. Now how did that get there?'

Behind him the door creaked slowly open. For a moment Jago stayed where he was, frozen with terror. He dropped the lid of the hamper and turned—to see Casey in the doorway. 'Ready, Mr Jago?'

'Casey! Don't ever do that to me again. If Chang caught me prying into his secrets ...'

'What were you after doing, sir?'

Jago decided to say nothing about the blood. Casey was panicky enough already. 'I had some idea the dummy might be a midget dressed up. But it's just an ordinary ventriloquist's doll.'

'Are we going to take a look down the cellar, Mr Jago —like you said?'

'Of course, Casey, of course. When I promise to do something, it gets done. Determination, Casey. Character. That's the secret of my success. We'll go and hunt for your ghost.' Outside Chang's dressing-room, Jago paused. There was something rather unattractive about the thought of poking about in the cellar. 'Tell you what, Casey, we'll go to my office and have a little drink before we start, eh? Maybe one kind of spirit will help us to deal with the other!'

The Doctor strode confidently through the swirling fog, Leela hurrying to keep up with him. 'Where are we going now, Doctor?'

'To the mortuary, the place where they keep the dead bodies. A doctor is going to examine the body of that prisoner.'

'Why? He is dead.'

'We may still be able to learn something more about *how* he died.'

Leela shook her head, baffled. There was no point

in worrying about the body of a dead enemy. Live ones were far more important. 'What is this Tong of the Black Scorpion, Doctor?'

'A Chinese secret society, fanatical followers of an ancient Chinese god called Weng-Chiang. They believe that one day he will return to rule the world.'

Leela paused, and looked over her shoulder. She had a kind of tingling sensation between her shoulder-blades—usually a sure sign she was being hunted. But the long dark street behind them seemed completely empty. She hurried after the Doctor.

(Behind her, a black-clad figure, almost invisible in the darkness, slipped out of an alleyway and followed soundlessly.)

Catching up with the Doctor, Leela asked, 'What is he like, this Weng-Chiang?'

'Not very pleasant company. They say he blew poisonous fumes from his mouth, and killed men with a great light that shone from his eyes.'

Leela was impressed. 'Magic?'

'Superstitious rubbish,' said the Doctor briefly. 'Ah, this looks like the place.' They had reached a long, low building, set back a little from the cobbled street, yellow light shining from its windows. A couple of steps led up to a central door. The Doctor flung it open, and ushered Leela inside.

(As the door closed behind them, a black-clad figure slipped out of the darkness, and peered cautiously through the window.)

Leela found herself in a place not unlike the police station they had just left. Whitewashed walls, a desk, wooden benches. This time there was something different, a pervading smell of disinfectant that hung on the air like a gas, and one end of the long bare room was concealed by screens.

The Doctor was talking to another of the blue

guards. 'You mean nothing's been done? Surely you got the Sergeant's message? He sent a note round with the body of the man.'

'We got the message right enough, sir!' said the policeman patiently. 'But Professor Litefoot is already doing a post mortem examination. A body was taken from the river, not half an hour ago.'

'Well, our case is far more urgent.' Brushing the attendant aside, the Doctor marched behind the screens. A body was laid out on a mortuary slab and a tall, greyhaired man with a beaky nose was holding a test tube up to the light, and frowning fiercely at it. 'Professor Litefoot, I presume?' said the Doctor cheerfully.

Litefoot glared at him. 'Who the devil are you, sir?'

'I'm the Doctor. I've come to help you.'

'When I need anyone's help in pathology, Doctor, I'll ask for it.' Ignoring the Doctor, Litefoot went on with his examination.

Professor Litefoot was a well-known local character. A member of a wealthy upper-class family, he could, if he wished, have had a fashionable practice in Harley Street. But after a spell in the Army, he had deliberately chosen to come and work at a hospital in London's East End. Here he could do real and useful work, instead of, as he put it himself, 'dosing a lot of silly women suffering from the vapours'. Worse still, he had taken the post of police pathologist, deliberately involving himself in the crime so common in the area. His aristocratic relations had long ago given up trying to make him see reason. Litefoot went his own way, and he always would.

Deliberately ignoring the Doctor's presence, Litefoot went on with his examination. He was frequently plagued by visiting dignitaries from Scotland Yard, the Home Office and various government Committees, and assumed the Doctor was another of their number. In Litefoot's experience, if you ignored these people they eventually went away. To his annoyance, the Doctor refused to go away, and began studying the body with almost professional interest. 'I thought the constable said this was a drowning case?'

'Body was fished from the river. Not drowned, though.'

'Attacked by some kind of animal too—*after* death.'

Litefoot looked at his visitor with new respect. 'That was my theory, too. But what kind of animal leaves marks like that?'

The Doctor studied the terrible wounds. 'Something with chisel-like incisor teeth. In other words, a rodent.'

'A rodent? Look at the *size* of those marks!'

'What was the actual cause of death?'

'That's another thing. *Not* drowning, and not these bites, either.' Litefoot pointed. 'The man was killed by a knife-blow to the heart.'

The Doctor glanced at Leela, who had followed him round the screen. 'It seems you were right after all.'

'About what?'

'The different sounds of death.' He turned to the policeman. 'Where are the man's clothes?'

'Here, sir.' The policeman indicated a shabby bundle on a table in the corner. 'No documents on the body, but we found this.' He picked up a big metal disc with a number stamped on it. 'Means he was a licensed cab driver. We'll be able to identify the poor chap by the number easy enough.'

'The body those men were carrying wore clothing much like this,' whispered Leela.

The Doctor picked up the shabby coat and held it up to the light. He plucked something from the coat between finger and thumb.

31

'What have you found, Doctor?' asked Litefoot curiously.

The Doctor held out his hand, a few coarse grey hairs in the palm. 'Rat's hairs.'

Litefoot stared. 'Do you know what you're saying?'

'I always know what I'm saying, Professor Litefoot. Others are sometimes a little slow to understand.'

'But the hairs on a rat must measure less than a quarter of an inch. These are nearly three inches long!'

The Doctor nodded. 'Interesting, isn't it?' He looked thoughtfully at Leela. 'You know, I've just remembered something else about Weng-Chiang.'

'What, Doctor?'

'He was the god of abundance,' said the Doctor slowly. 'When he wanted to, he could make things grow very big.' He took a policeman's lantern from a shelf on the wall. 'I'll borrow this if I may,' he said, and made for the door.

Leela followed him. 'Where are we going, Doctor?'

The Doctor waved her back. 'You're not going anywhere, Leela. I want you to stay here. *I'm* going out to look for a giant rat!'

# 4

# The Monster in the Tunnel

Closing the mortuary door behind him, the Doctor strode rapidly along the deserted street. A black-clad figure slid round the corner of the building and set off in pursuit.

As he padded silently after the Doctor, the Tong assassin slipped a hatchet from beneath his tunic. Truly Weng-Chiang was smiling upon him this night. He had been ordered to kill the two strangers, quietly without fuss. When they had entered the place where there were more accursed police he thought he had missed his chance. Now the tall man had come out—alone and unprotected. When the man was dead, he would return and wait for the girl.

The tall Doctor paused by a lamp-post before a row of terraced houses. There would never be a better chance. Drawing back his arm, the assassin hurled the deadly hatchet with all his force . . . just as the Doctor took a step forward. The hatchet whizzed past his ear and thudded into a doorpost beside his head.

The Doctor whirled round. The assassin was standing motionless on the pavement some way behind him. He was quite still, as if paralysed by the failure of his attack. The Doctor wrenched the hatchet from the doorpost and strode grimly towards his attacker. 'I take it you were trying to attract my attention?'

The assassin did not move or speak. He stared bulging-eyed at the Doctor for a moment, then pitched forward, falling face down on to the cobbles. Leela stepped from the doorway behind him, tucking a small pointed object back into the waist-band of her suit.

'Leela, what is that?' demanded the Doctor sternly.

'A Janis thorn.'

The Janis thorn was a product of Leela's native planet. It produced instant paralysis, followed by inevitable death. 'I thought I told you never to use those things again.'

'He was trying to *kill* you, Doctor.'

The Doctor considered. He was against killing of course. But he was also against being killed. 'All right,' he said ungraciously. 'Since you're here, you'd better come along.'

Leela grinned, and followed him down the street.

He led her to a road junction, close to the spot where they had first seen the four Chinese with the body. Kneeling on the cobbles, he shone his lantern on to the round manhole cover.

Leela looked down at it. 'What is it, Doctor?'

'This is where they took the body when they disappeared so suddenly.'

'Where does it lead?'

'Into the Thames, eventually. All the sewers must be connected.' The Doctor was busily prising up the manhole cover. It landed on the cobbles with an echoing clang, revealing a dark opening with a ladder bolted to the side. Swinging nimbly on to the ladder, the Doctor disappeared into the darkness, and a moment later, Leela followed him.

They climbed down into a dank and echoing tunnel, through the centre of which flowed an evil-smelling stream. Lantern held high, the Doctor moved ahead, Leela close behind him. She felt she had never been in a more unpleasant place. 'What are we looking for, Doctor?'

'Anything we can find.' The Doctor shone the lantern down the tunnel, and Leela caught a glimpse of

34

bright-eyed, grey shapes scurrying away into the darkness.

'What are those creatures?'

'Rats.'

'They don't look too dangerous.'

'Not singly, perhaps. But they hunt in packs, and they're very cunning. Besides if my theory is correct, we may well run into something rather——'

The Doctor broke off. From the darkness ahead came a high squealing sound, and the patter of hundreds of scampering feet. The beam of the lantern showed a flood of grey shapes rushing towards them.

Leela grasped the Doctor's arm. 'We must flee. The rat creatures are massing to attack us.'

The Doctor stood his ground. 'I don't think so. They're running *from* something.' Sure enough, the stream of grey shapes flowed by ignoring them. There was a moment of silence and then another sound, like the squealing of rats magnified a hundred times.

The Doctor raised his lantern. Scurrying down the tunnel towards them was a enormous rat.

Leela gasped. The creature was huge and savage, at least twice as big as a man. It paused, red eyes blinking in the light, then with a trumpeting scream it charged them, the yellow fangs bared in fury.

'Run!' yelled the Doctor. They turned and fled, back down the sewer tunnel. When they reached the ladder, Leela clambered up with frantic speed. The Doctor paused and hurled his lantern at the huge grey shape rushing out of the darkness. As the Doctor scrambled up the ladder, the lantern smashed on the stone pavings and burst into a sheet of flame. The monster retreated with a scream of pain.

The Doctor shot out of the manhole like a jack-in-the-box, slammed the cover back in place and sat on it gasping for breath. From below came a muffled roar, as a vast bulk hurled itself against the ladder.

Leela looked disapprovingly at the Doctor. 'That was foolishness. We might have been killed.'

'Well, at least we know I was on the right track,' said the Doctor defensively. 'What a whopper, eh? Ten feet, from whiskers to tail!'

'We should have taken weapons.'

'What kind of weapons? You'd need a cannon to stop that brute.'

'Shall we tell the blue guards?'

'The police? They'd never believe us. At most they'd send a sanitary inspector—and he might get a nasty shock!'

The roaring below had died away. The Doctor got cautiously to his feet. 'You know, Leela, I think that thing was a kind of guard, to keep people like us away. So there must be something worth guarding down there, eh? Come on!'

'*Now* where are we going?'

'Back to the police station. I want to see if they've got a plan of the sewers.'

When they reached the station, Sergeant Kyle listened to the Doctor's request with his usual air of weary patience. 'A plan of the sewers, Doctor? We don't keep one here, I'm afraid. Why do you ask? If you've any information——'

'At the moment, Sergeant, we're looking for information ourselves.'

Kyle stroked his moustache. 'I see,' he said heavily, though he didn't see at all. 'I do have a message for you though, sir. From Professor Litefoot. He'd like to see you at the mortuary as soon as possible.'

'Still there, is he?'

'Oh yes, sir, he's still there. Apparently they found another body, soon after you left. Another Chinese. He was in the street, not far away.'

'Very convenient,' said the Doctor blandly.

'Very mysterious, sir. Don't suppose you know anything about it?'

'Of course we do,' said Leela helpfully. 'As a matter of fact, I——'

'Thank you for the message, Sergeant,' interrupted the Doctor hastily. 'We'll go and see Professor Litefoot at once.'


It took quite a few little drinks before Jago and Casey were ready to go looking down the dark cellar. But they screwed up their courage at last, and pleasantly aglow with brandy, they made their way down to the huge cellar that ran underneath the stage. 'Black as Newgate's knocker down here, Mr Jago,' said Casey, as they came down the cellar stairs.

Jago shone his lantern. The cellar was piled high with all kinds of junk, accumulated during the long life of the theatre. There were boxes, crates, baskets, coils of rope, abandoned stage props. Jago decided he really must get it cleared out some day.

Casey pointed to an arched recess in the wall. 'That's where I saw it, Mr Jago.'

'Flickering shadows,' said Jago, trying to convince himself he wasn't frightened. 'Just a trick of the light.'

'Shadows don't groan,' whispered Casey sinisterly. 'Shadows don't clank chains and moan, like all the tormented souls in hell.'

Jago held up his lantern and advanced determinedly towards the recess. He jumped back as a demoniacally grinning face jumped out of the darkness. 'There's your ghost.' He held the lantern up to a carved Indian totem pole leaning against the wall. 'Six-gun Sadie and her Wild West Troupe left it behind. Lombard Street to a china orange that's what frightened you.'

Casey said stubbornly, 'Weren't that old thing. I saw a ghost—and heard it too, I tell you.'

'Look,' said Jago patiently, 'the old Fleet River runs under here. Running water makes all kinds of noises . . .' He paused and picked up something from the floor. 'What's this, Casey, you been bringing a lady friend down here? Lady's glove, monogrammed "E.B.".' He slipped the glove into his pocket. 'Come on, Casey, we've wasted enough time on your spook.' He led the way upstairs, and ushered the still-grumbling Casey to the stage door. 'Now, straight home with you, Casey, and no lingering on the way. Someone might mistake you for a pretty girl. Doubtless I shall descry your lugubrious lineaments at the crepuscular hour.'

'What's that, sir?'

Jago gave him a friendly shove. 'See you in the morning!'

'You're a card, Mr Jago. A card and a half, you are.' Still chuckling, Casey went off down the alley.

Locking the stage door Jago turned—to find Chang looming over him. His heart gave a great leap, and he caught his breath. 'By Jiminy, you gave me a shock, Mr Chang. I thought you'd gone.'

'I had, Mr Jago. But I have returned to see you.'

'Nothing wrong, I hope?'

'Be so kind as to step into my dressing-room.'

Jago put on his most jovial manner as he entered the little dressing-room. 'If it's about your contract, Mr Chang, let me say right away that I plan to offer you better terms. We've been attracting such good houses, it's the least I can do.'

Chang made no reply. He stared at Jago, eyes glittering hypnotically. Jago stumbled on. 'I venture to say no management in London could offer an artiste better terms. What would you say to an extra two per

cent of the gross, Mr Chang? I think that's fair ...
that's fair ...' Jago's voice faltered and died away.

'Hear me, Jago,' said Chang softly. 'You will forget
everything about Buller, the cab driver who came here
earlier. You did not see him.'

'I did not see him.'

'You will go to your office, and remember only that
you have just said good night to Casey.'

'I have just said good night to Casey.'

'Good. Now go.'

Jago turned at once and walked from the room. A
few minutes later he found himself sitting down at his
desk, going through the accounts for the evening. He
rubbed his hand over his eyes. He'd felt a bit queer for
a moment. Must have been old Casey, with all that
nonsense about ghosts in the cellar. Lighting a fresh
cigar, Jago went on with his work.

Chang made his way through the darkened theatre
and down the cellar steps. He went to the recess where
Casey had seen his 'ghost', took an iron bar from its
hiding place in the corner, and knocked three times
on the stone flags. There was a grinding sound, and
a flagstone slid back revealing a wooden ladder that
led down into darkness. Chang started to descend.

The ladder ended in a vaulted chamber deep below
the theatre. It was furnished with a strange mixture of
Chinese-style drapes and hangings, and ultra-modern
scientific equipment. A shallow culvert ran along the
far side of the room. It ended in a barred arch, through
which could be heard the sound of running water.

Waiting at the foot of the ladder was a strange and
terrifying figure. It was tall and thin, dressed in close-
fitting black garments and an all-enveloping black
cloak. A soft black-leather mask covered the face,
which was overshadowed by a broad-brimmed black
hat. Chang dropped from the ladder, and bowed low

before the sinister apparition. This was his lord and master Greel, living embodiment of the god Weng-Chiang.

Greel spoke in a dry rasping voice, each word forced out with painful effort. 'You are late.'

'I am sorry, Lord. I was delayed.'

Suddenly Greel staggered, supporting himself against the wall with a long-taloned hand. Chang looked up in concern. 'You should not go out tonight, Lord.'

Greel hobbled painfully across the chamber, and sank wearily on to a stool. 'I must. Tonight, *every* night, until the Time Cabinet is found.'

'You are ill.'

'I am *dying*, Chang. You must bring another linnet to my cage.' Greel waved towards a sinister-looking complex of machinery that stood against the far wall. Its dominant feature was a transparent cabinet from the top of which were suspended two golden metal balls.

'Already, Lord?' whispered Chang. There was fear in his voice. 'But only yesterday ...'

'My disease grows worse,' rasped Greel. 'Each distillation has less effect than the one before.'

'But Lord, each missing girl increases the panic, and the suspicion. Even tonight, there was danger.' Hurriedly Chang told his master of Buller's suspicions, of the murder on the way to the police station, and his hypnotising of Jago.

Greel showed little appreciation of the many efforts of his servant. 'I have given you mental powers undreamed of in this primitive century, Chang. What have you to fear from these savages?'

'True, Lord: I read their minds with ease. But tonight there was a stranger, one whose thoughts were hidden from me.'

40

'Describe him.'

'He calls himself the Doctor. Tall with wide, pale eyes, and hair that curls close like the ram. He asks questions, many questions.'

Greel made a dismissive gesture. 'A Time Agent would not ask questions, Chang. A Time Agent would *know*.'

Chang was not convinced. 'I sensed danger from him and from his companion. I have ordered your servants to slay them.'

'Opium-addicted scum of the Tongs! They are all bunglers. You should have seen to it yourself.'

'I will do so, Lord, should he trouble us further.'

Greel wrapped his cloak about him, and made for the ladder. 'We are wasting time. Come, we must begin our task.'


Outside the theatre a carriage was waiting, a black-clad, pigtailed driver at the reins. Soon Greel and his servant Chang were rattling through the cobbled streets on their terrifying errand.

# 5

## The Quest of Greel

Professor Litefoot rolled down his sleeves and slipped into the coat held for him by a respectful constable. 'I must confess, Doctor, this thing has me beaten. One of those Chinese was poisoned orally, the other pricked by some poisoned instrument. Different poisons in each case. Understand you suggested scorpion venom, for the first chap?'

The Doctor passed Litefoot his overcoat. 'It's a possibility. Highly concentrated of course.'

'And the second?'

The Doctor coughed and shot Leela a warning glance. 'I really couldn't say.'

Litefoot seemed positively stimulated by the dramatic events of the evening. 'What a night, eh?' he said gleefully. 'Most of the corpses around here are very dull. Now I've got a couple of mysteriously dead Chinese and a poor perisher who was bitten by a giant rat after being stabbed by a midget!'

Leela stared at him. 'A midget?'

Litefoot made an upward stabbing gesture. 'Angle of the wound—sorry, my dear.'

'What for?'

Litefoot looked embarrassed. 'For mentioning such indelicate topics in the presence of a lady.'

Leela gave the Doctor a baffled look. 'Does he mean me?'

'I think so,' said the Doctor solemnly.

Leela turned back to Litefoot. 'You can tell the height of the attacker by the way the blade was thrust?'

'Quite so, my dear. But you mustn't bother your pretty head ...'

'We were always taught to strike upwards under the breast-bone when aiming for the heart.'

'Well, upon my soul, young lady ...'

The Doctor took Litefoot aside. 'Raised by savages,' he whispered. 'Found floating down the Amazon in a hatbox!'

'A hatbox?'

Before the Doctor had a chance to elaborate on his story, they were interrupted by the return of the police constable who had been on duty earlier. He was strangely bright and cheerful, despite the foggy night. 'Still here then, Professor? I've just traced your cab driver for you.' He produced his notebook with a flourish. 'Name of Alfred Buller, of Fourteen, Fish Lane, this parish.'

'Splendid work, Constable Quick,' said Litefoot heartily. 'The Coroner will want the details for his report. Did someone identify the clothing?'

P.C. Quick produced his notebook. 'Mother-in-law, Mrs Nellie Gossett, of the same address. Deceased had lived with her since his marriage six months ago.'

The Doctor's nostrils twitched. A familiar odour had come into the room with P.C. Quick—a faint but unmistakable whiff of gin. 'You stayed for a drink with Mrs Gossett, I think, Constable. What else did she have to say?'

Guiltily Quick wiped his moustache with the back of his hand. 'Well as the bearer of sad tidings, sir, I did share a glass or two, just to help the poor old dear get over the shock.' He consulted his notebook. 'She said the deceased had been in a state all day, owing to the fact that his wife, Emma Buller, didn't come home last night. Deceased had several drinks then went off to the Palace Theatre where he believed his wife was to

43

be found. Mrs Gossett said he went off making horrible threats.'

The Doctor rubbed his chin. 'Thank you, that's very interesting.'

Professor Litefoot didn't seem to think so. 'Just put the relevant information in your report, Constable. Clearly the man got stupidly drunk, then got into a fight with a dwarf!'

'Yessir, very good sir,' said Quick woodenly, and disappeared to make out his report.

Litefoot turned to the Doctor and Leela. 'A busy night does wonders for my appetite. I'd be honoured if you'd both come home and share a spot of supper with me.'

The Doctor stood lost in thought, and didn't seem to hear the Professor's invitation. Leela nudged him in the ribs, and he looked up. 'What's that Professor, supper? I'd be delighted.'

Litefoot had a hackney-cab waiting outside, and soon they were rattling over the cobbles. It was very late now. The pubs and theatres had closed, the last revellers had made their way home and the foggy streets were dark and empty.

Litefoot produced a huge curved pipe, and began trying to light it with a succession of matches. 'Normally the police would have these cases cleared up in no time. But with these Chinese involved—different kettle of fish, what?'

Leela had been watching Litefoot's efforts with fascination. 'Why are you making a fire in your mouth?'

''Pon my soul, girl, haven't you ever seen a pipe before?'

The Doctor smiled. 'People don't smoke where Leela comes from. In any case, it's a most unhealthy habit.'

'Quite agree,' said Litefoot, taking another puff at his pipe. 'Yes, as I was saying, they're a mysterious lot, the Chinese. I never came anywhere near understanding 'em, and I grew up in China.'

'How did that come about?' asked the Doctor curiously.

'Father was an army man. Brigadier, actually. Went out with the punitive expedition in 1860. Stayed on in Peking, as a palace attaché. Poor old buffer died out there in the end. Fireworks at the funeral, I remember.' Litefoot puffed meditatively at his pipe. 'Odd custom. Odd sort of people altogether.'

The Doctor reached up and rapped sharply on the roof of the cab, to signal to the driver to stop. He swung his long legs out of the carriage and stood beside it looking thoughtfully up at them. 'Evil spirits,' he said suddenly. 'They use fireworks to frighten off evil spirits.'

'I know that,' spluttered Litefoot. 'What's the matter, Doctor?'

The Doctor ignored him. 'You go on with the Professor, Leela. I'll join you later.'

'Where are you going?'

'To the Palace Theatre. All right, Cabbie, drive on!'

The Doctor slapped the side of the carriage, and before Leela could protest further, the carriage was jolting on its way, leaving the Doctor behind.

Litefoot shook his head. 'Extraordinary feller. How can he join us later? He doesn't know my address.'

'Four, Ranskill Gardens,' said Leela promptly. 'He heard you tell the driver.'

Litefoot stared admiringly at her. 'Gad! That's amazing. You're as sharp as a trout.'

'Trout?'

45

'It's a kind of fish, my dear . . .'

The hackney-carriage rattled on its way.

Jago had just finished totting up the night's takings when he heard a persistent banging. He climbed wearily to his feet, went along the corridor and opened the stage door. A very tall man slipped nimbly through the gap, and stood beaming at him. 'Thank you very much. Terrible fog tonight.' Calmly the stranger closed the stage door behind him. 'Are you the manager?'

'Manager and owner, sir. Henry Gordon Jago, at the end of a long, hard day. So if you will kindly state your business——'

The Doctor seized Jago's hand and shook it warmly. 'A very great pleasure, Mr Jago. I'm the Doctor. How do you do?'

'The Doctor?'

'Exactly.'

Jago nodded understandingly. 'Aha! Now I've rumbled your game. I admire your brass, sir, but it won't do. Call back on Saturday. Auditions commence at ten sharp, supporting acts booked for one week only.'

Suddenly the Doctor realised that Jago had taken him for a music-hall performer trying to get a booking. He smiled delightedly. 'Just one moment, Mr Jago.' The Doctor snatched the white handkerchief from Jago's breast-pocket and flourished it. Immediately the handkerchief turned into a string of flags of all nations. Still beaming, the Doctor crumpled the flags into a ball, and they turned into a live dove, which fluttered away down the corridor.

Jago shook his head. 'I'm sorry, Doctor, we've already got a very good magician.'

The Doctor gave a disappointed sigh. 'Dramatic recitations? Tap dancing?' he said hopefully. 'I can play the Trumpet Voluntary in a tank of live goldfish!'

Jago waved him towards the door. 'Don't bother about coming back on Saturday ...'

The Doctor grinned, and abandoned his masquerade. 'As a matter of fact, Mr Jago, I didn't come here for a job. I came to ask you a few questions—about a cab driver by the name of Buller.'

Immediately Jago's face went blank. 'Never heard of him.'

The Doctor looked hard at Jago. It was as if a shutter had suddenly slammed down behind Jago's eyes. 'I'm also a master hypnotist,' said the Doctor sternly. 'How long since *you* were under the influence?'

Jago was indignant. 'Me, sir? I am a man of character and determination. The Rock of Gibraltar would be more easily ... more easily ...' Jago's voice faltered. The wide staring eyes of the stranger held him transfixed.

'As I thought,' said the Doctor gently. 'Now, what was your last order?'

'To remember nothing since I said good night to Casey,' said Jago tonelessly.

The Doctor spoke in a low, compelling voice. 'Henry Gordon Jago, I want you to tell me everything you were ordered to forget. You will remember everything when I count to three. One ... two ... three!'

Jago blinked. 'I tell you sir, I have a will of iron ... What the blazes were we talking about? Oh yes, that fellow Buller. Burst in and accosted Mr Chang between houses. Something to do with a lady called Emma.'

'His wife, Emma Buller. She disappeared last night. What's the matter?'

47

Jago was staring blankly at him. 'Emma Buller.' He fished a crumpled glove from his pocket, and handed it to the Doctor.

The Doctor read the monogrammed initials. 'E.B. Where did you find this?'

'In the cellar. I say, are you from the police?'

'I'm helping them. Now, Mr Jago, I want to take a look at this cellar of yours.'


While Litefoot's carriage carried the Professor and Leela back towards his neat suburban villa, another carriage was rattling through the deserted streets not far away. Inside were Greel, Li H'sen Chang—and Mr Sin. Greel was holding a saucer-shaped crystal pendant in his hands. He stared hard at the pendant, and sighed with disappointment. 'You are certain these are *different* streets?'

'The driver knows his orders, Lord. Every night we search a new area.'

'Yes! And for how much longer? How many more nights must I spend in this endless quest?'

'Patience, Lord. The city is large. But we know that the Time Cabinet is here, in the house of some infidel. We *shall* recover it.'

'I grow weary, Chang. Weary!' Greel slumped disconsolately back in his seat.

Chang looked worriedly at the black-masked visage of his master. It is no small responsibility to be the servant of a dying god. He made his voice encouraging. 'Tomorrow I will bring you two new donors. Young and vigorous girls. The distillation of their life-essences will quickly restore your powers.'

Greel nodded wearily. Chang looked sadly at his master. Greel was weakening fast. Unless the Time

Cabinet was found soon, it would be too late to save him—however many young girls were sacrificed.

Jago held up his lantern. 'The glove was lying just here, Doctor. I came down to reassure Casey, my care-taker. He's taken to seeing ghosts lately.' Jago jumped back. Disturbed by the light of his lantern, a huge round black shape had scuttled away into a dark corner. 'What a spider, eh? That must be the grand-dad of them all.'

'It's a money spider,' said the Doctor absently. He shone his lantern around the cellar.

Jago laughed nervously. 'Money spider, eh? Don't kill it, Doctor, it'll bring us luck. Why's it so big though?'

'Genetic disruption,' said the Doctor to himself. 'Affecting the size of the local fauna—like that rat. Emanations of some kind ... but where are they com-ing from, eh?' He swung round on Jago. 'Is there anything under us here, Mr Jago?'

'Under here? Where we're standing you mean? Well, this theatre was built on the site of a much older building. And they say the course of the old Fleet River lies right under these foundations.'

The Doctor nodded happily. 'Splendid. Now we're getting somewhere!' He knelt down and examined the flagstones, rapping hard at different points, and listen-ing to the resulting sound. 'If there is an entrance here, it's expertly hidden ...'

Jago looked nervously round the gloomy cellar. The abandoned theatre-props seemed to form strange shapes in the darkness. Suddenly a glowing point of light appeared in the arched recess. It grew and grew until there was a floating shape inside the arch, a horrible glowing figure with a skull-like face. 'Look out, Doctor,' yelled Jago. 'It's the ghost!'

Slowly the hideously glowing figure floated towards them.

# 6

## The Tong Attacks

The Doctor studied the approaching phantom with scientific detachment. 'Interesting,' he murmured. 'Extremely interesting.'

Jago couldn't quite manage the Doctor's calm. His nerve broke and he turned and ran. Unfortunately his foot became tangled in a trailing rope. Convinced the ghost had caught him, Jago gave a yell of terror, wrenched himself free and crashed head-first into a stone pillar, knocking himself senseless.

The Doctor knelt at his side. Jago lay unconscious, a bruised forehead. Glancing over his shoulder, the Doctor saw the phantom hover, fade and vanish. He looked down at the unconscious Jago. 'Come on, Rock of Gibraltar,' he murmured. Hoisting Jago on to his shoulder, he carried him out of the cellar.

Litefoot ushered Leela into his dining-room. He was a little dubious about the propriety of being with an unchaperoned young female so late at night. But he'd already seen enough of Leela to realise that ideas of polite behaviour meant little to her.

Leela looked curiously round the sitting-room. To her it seemed cluttered, overcrowded with heavy furniture and a variety of fussy ornaments. She knew too little of Earth's culture to realise that two distinct styles were mingled in the room. The mahogany dining table, the ornately carved chairs, the overstuffed armchairs and divans were all the standard furnishings of a prosperous Victorian home. But the ornate tapestries, the lacquer-work cabinets and the strangely-carved jade ornaments came from a far older culture. They were all souvenirs of China, brought home from Peking. The pride of the collection stood in a corner of the room. It was a huge black cabinet, decorated with ornate golden scrolls. It was roughly the size and shape of the Doctor's TARDIS.

Litefoot was lifting covers from a side table. 'Mrs Hudson, my housekeeper, always leaves me a cold collation when I'm working late. Now, let's see what we have here. Ham, roast beef, chicken, tongue ... and those look like quail, unless I'm much mistaken.' Litefoot rubbed his hands. He had a handsome private income, and was accustomed to doing himself well. 'Perhaps we needn't wait for your friend the Doctor, my dear. Just help yourself, will you? Plates at the end of the table. I'll put a knob or two on the fire.'

While Litefoot busied himself with coal scuttle and tongs, Leela tore off a chunk of beef with her fingers, tasted it and nodded appreciatively. Litefoot straightened up in time to see her seize the joint in both hands and tear at it with strong white teeth. He gulped. 'Er, would you care for a knife and fork?'

Leela saw a carving knife on one of the platters. She snatched it up and ran a thumb appreciatively along the edge ... 'Ah ... it's a good knife.' She started sawing chunks from the joint and stuffing them into her mouth. She looked at Litefoot in surprise. 'Aren't you hungry?'

A Victorian gentleman to the core, Litefoot was well aware of the first rule of true hospitality. A guest must never be made to feel awkward or uncomfortable. Manfully, he snatched up a whole boiled ham and began biting into it. Leela smiled happily, and went on with her meal. From somewhere nearby came the faint sound of a passing carriage ...

Greel's eyes were half closed, his head slumped forward, as the carriage jolted through the night streets on its endless journey. He was beginning to lose hope, to feel he must die here in this barbaric century. Would he never be able to return to his own place and time? Not until the Time Cabinet was found ...

Suddenly his eyes snapped open, and he sat bolt upright. The crystal pendant, dangling unregarded from his hands, was beginning to *glow* ... 'Stop!' he called. 'Our search is over. The Time Cabinet is *here*— somewhere among these dwellings ...'

The carriage clattered to a halt, and Chang jumped down, assisting Greel to climb painfully after him. They stood in a tree-lined suburban street. Greel swung round in a circle, and when the pendant began to glow more brightly, he moved slowly forwards.

The pendant led them straight towards a solid Victorian villa, set well back from the road, behind a front garden filled with dense shrubbery. 'It is here,' croaked Greel. 'The Time Cabinet is *here*, in this house!' Relief left him suddenly weak and he staggered and almost fell.

Chang caught his Master by the arm and steadied him. 'You grow weak, Lord. Leave the rest to your servants and go back to your abode.'

The eyes behind the mask glowed with an obsessive passion. 'The cabinet ... Chang. I must have the cabinet.'

'Rest, Lord, and I will bring the cabinet to you ...'

Greel's bony claw gripped his arm. 'Very well. But do not fail me, now, Chang. *Do not fail me!*'

Greel climbed into the carriage. At a sign from

Chang, the Chinese driver cracked the whip and drove away. Mr Sin on his arm, Chang moved cautiously towards the house.

The Doctor held a glass of water to Jago's lips. 'Here, sit up and drink this. You'll soon feel better.'

Fearfully Jago opened his eyes and found to his relief that he was out of the cellar, propped up against the wall in the corridor backstage. He swigged gratefully at the water, and looked up at the Doctor. 'The ghost! I saw it. Oh, Casey forgive me, I saw it.'

The Doctor helped him to sit up. 'What you saw, Mr Jago, was a hologram.'

'A grinning skull,' gasped Jago. 'A monster ten foot high. I always knew there was something unnatural about that cellar.'

'There's nothing unnatural about the holograph technique,' said the Doctor severely. 'Simply a way of using a laser-beam to project a three-dimensional image. What *is* unnatural is the use of the technique in this century. It hasn't been discovered yet!'

Jago struggled to his feet. 'Oh, I see,' he said blankly. Suddenly he caught a glimpse of a dark shape, moving into the wings.

'Someone's moving! Over there on the stage.'

'Stay there. I'll go and take a look.' The Doctor disappeared into the wings.

Behind the lowered curtain, the stage was in utter darkness. The Doctor saw a black shape dodge in front of the curtains. He followed, and found himself on the narrow strip of stage on the other side. In front of him were the footlights, the darkness of the orchestra pit and the rows and rows of empty seats. Everything was dark and silent.

The Doctor stood listening. He heard a faint scuffling from the orchestra pit, and immediately jumped down. A fleeting glimpse of a black-cloaked figure— and an orchestra chair smashed down, knocking him off his feet.

The chair was spindly, and the Doctor got his arms up in time to protect his head. Struggling to his feet, he saw his attacker disappear behind the curtain, and staggered in pursuit.

Once again his attacker had vanished. The Doctor listened, and heard a scrabbling sound from the other side of the stage. He crossed over. An iron ladder, bolted to the wall, led upward into darkness. Guessing his attacker was somewhere above him, the Doctor started to climb. Something heavy hurtled out of the darkness, knocking him clean off the ladder. An open costume-basket broke his fall, and disentangling himself from a pile of draperies, the Doctor saw that the missile had been a stuffed tiger's head. He climbed out of the basket and started climbing again.

The ladder took him up to a kind of catwalk, high above the stage. All around were the various ropes and counterweights by means of which the backdrops to the acts were raised and lowered. The Doctor was edging his way along the narrow walk-way when a huge black shape, swinging on one of the dangling ropes, hurtled out of the darkness like a giant bat, aimed a kick that missed by inches and disappeared into the darkness on the other side of the stage. The Doctor ran in pursuit. The figure landed on the catwalk and disappeared into the dark area behind it.

By the time he reached the other side of the catwalk, his attacker was nowhere to be seen. The Doctor wondered if his quarry was already climbing the ladder. A black shape appeared behind him, and thrust him over the edge of the catwalk with a savage heave.

The Doctor hurtled downwards, frantically reaching out for something to hold on to. He managed to grasp the edge of the velvet side-curtain, and hung on desperately. The curtain began to tear beneath his weight ... As he struggled to improve his grip, the Doctor saw his enemy slide down a dangling rope to the stage below, and run towards the cellar steps. The curtain gave way, and the Doctor tumbled downwards in a tangle of red velvet.

Jago meanwhile had got to his feet and was staggering gallantly to the Doctor's aid. He reached the stage just in time to be knocked down by the black-cloaked figure. By the time he had picked himself up, it had disappeared down the cellar steps. Struggling free of the torn curtain the Doctor followed it, and Jago hurried after him.

He found the Doctor at the bottom of the steps, looking thoughtfully round the empty cellar. 'What happened?' panted Jago. 'Who was that?'

'I haven't the faintest idea. He didn't introduce himself. Anyway, he seems to have gone back to his rats.'

Jago stared at the cellar floor. 'I'll get the police down here with picks and shovels,' he said fiercely.

'Our reclusive phantom would vanish straight away, I'm afraid.' The Doctor laid a hand on Jago's shoulder. 'We shall tackle this together, Mr Jago.'

Jago winced, but tried to sound enthusiastic. 'Yes, indeed, Doctor. What *are* you going to do next?'

'Think!' said the Doctor solemnly. 'Now if you'll excuse me, I have a supper engagement!'


Leela tossed aside a well-gnawed bone, and wiped her greasy hands on her suit. 'Napkin?' suggested Litefoot tactfully. He passed one to Leela, and took one himself. Dabbing at his moustache, Litefoot wandered over to the window. 'Doctor's a long time. I hope he did note the address.' He opened the long velvet curtains and peered out. 'Great Scott!'

'What is it?'

'There's someone watching the house.' He pointed. 'Look, over there in the shrubbery.'

Leela looked out, but saw only the thick bushes in the dark front garden. 'Are you sure, Professor?'

'Saw him duck back into the shrubbery, just as I looked out. Chinese, I think.' Litefoot went to a bureau drawer and took out a heavy revolver. 'Well, whoever he is, I'll give him more than he bargained for. Wait here, my dear.'

Revolver in hand, Litefoot marched determinedly down the hall and out of the front door. He had seen service on the North-West Frontier in his Army days. No Chinese bandit was going to rob him without a fight.

He paused on the front steps and looked round. There was no one in sight. Revolver in hand, he made for the place where he'd seen the lurking figure. No one there. 'Sneaked round the back to look for an open window,' thought Litefoot. 'With any luck, I'll catch him in the act.' Revolver levelled, he crept cautiously round the side of the house.

In the dining-room, Leela waited. Had Litefoot really seen something, or was it all imagination? She was about to go out and look for him when she heard the front door open. 'Is that you, Professor?' she called.

Litefoot's cheerful voice came back. 'It's all right, my dear, nobody out there now. I've been all round the house. Fellow must have seen me coming and——'

There was a thud and a muffled groan. Then silence.

'Professor?' called Leela. There was no reply. The dining-room door swung silently open. A strange little figure stood in the doorway. It wore silk jacket and trousers and a little round cap, and its Oriental face stared impassively at her. In its hand gleamed a long pointed knife, held point-upwards. Leela backed cautiously away. Her instinct told her that despite its lack of size, the thing was deadly dangerous.

The hand with the knife came up, and the manikin stalked slowly towards her.

# 7

## The Lair of Weng-Chiang

Leela covered the distance to the dining table in a single backwards leap. Snatching up a carving knife she turned to the attack.

The manikin was still moving forward. Leela hefted the knife to judge the balance, shifted her grip to the blade then threw with all her strength. The knife spun in the air and thudded into the manikin's throat.

The manikin stopped for a moment, then shuffled forward again. Leela felt a chill of superstitious terror. She feared no living enemy—but now she was being hunted by something that could not be killed.

Knife in hand, the sinister little figure shuffled forward.

Just inside the open doorway of the house, Chang stood waiting for Mr Sin to complete his work. In his hand he held Litefoot's revolver, and the Professor's unconscious body lay at his feet. Suddenly Chang heard the crunch of footsteps on the gravel path. He ducked back into the doorway and peered out. The Doctor was strolling up the front path towards the house. Chang raised the revolver...

Step by step the manikin backed Leela into a corner. She could retreat no further. One more step and it would be close enough to use the knife.

Tensing her muscles, Leela took a flying leap forward, clean over the manikin's head. It slashed up at her, but missed. She rolled on to the dining table and jumped to her feet. The manikin had swung round to resume its remorseless pursuit.

Leela ran the length of the dining table and dived head-first for the curtained window ...

Leela exploded through the window with a crash of shattered glass. The Doctor swung round and Chang fired—and missed.

The Doctor ran to Leela, and yanked her into the cover of the shrubbery. The revolver boomed again, and a shot whistled over their heads. The Doctor and Leela instinctively dropped to the ground, and wriggled backwards into deeper cover.

Revolver raised, Chang crouched by the door. He peered into the darkness, but there was nothing to be seen. 'Sin,' he called, and the manikin stalked out of the dining-room towards him.

'Where's Litefoot?' whispered the Doctor.

'In the hall, I think. He went out to look for an enemy outside the window. They must have ambushed him when he got back.'

'And then you jumped through the window?'

'I *had* to. There was this—*thing* ...'

Before Leela could explain, the Doctor whispered, 'Stay here.' He slipped away through the shrubbery.

As soon as Mr Sin was near enough, Chang snatched him up and began backing away from the house.

The Doctor forced the kitchen window and climbed swiftly through.

Crouching in the shrubbery, Leela heard the clatter of hooves in the road. A carriage came tearing along and stopped outside the house. Chang ran down the front path, Mr Sin in his arms. He jumped into the carriage and it sped away.

Unable to bear the thought of their enemy escaping, Leela acted purely by instinct. She dashed after the carriage and leaped for the back step, clinging on as the carriage rattled away. It vanished from sight just as the Doctor ran through the house and out on to the front step. He looked round in astonishment. Chang had gone, and there was no sign of Leela. Only Litefoot was left, groaning feebly just inside the door.

Reflecting that this seemed to be his night for lugging bodies about, the Doctor picked Litefoot up and carried him into the dining-room. He put him on the couch, fetched water and a towel from the back kitchen, and bathed the Professor's forehead until he recovered consciousness. Litefoot came round with an indignant groan. 'The sheer criminal effrontery of it! Things have come to a pretty pass when ruffians attack a man in his own home.'

'*Chinese* ruffians, by any chance, Professor?'

'That's right. I wonder what they intended.'

The Doctor looked round the cluttered room. 'Robbery, perhaps?'

'It's very probable. I've quite a few valuable things here. That K'ang-hsi vase, for instance. Family brought that back from Peking. Or that Chinese cabinet.'

The Doctor went over to the cabinet and examined it. He tried the door, but it refused to move.

'I'm afraid it doesn't open. I spent ages looking for a secret spring, but it's no use.'

'Fused molecules, Professor.'

'No, no, Doctor. Lacquered bronze.'

The cabinet seemed to fascinate the Doctor. 'You're *sure* this is from *this* planet?'

'Of course it is. It comes from Peking—a gift from the Emperor himself.'

The Doctor was staring into space. 'Then what was a piece of technology as advanced as this doing in nineteenth-century China?' He stared intensely at Litefoot. 'Of course! That must be the answer ...'

Litefoot dabbed the bruise on his forehead. 'What *are* you babbling about, Doctor?'

'Weng-Chiang!'

Litefoot groaned. 'Not him again.'

'As soon as it's light, Professor, we must try to find Leela. I think she followed our Chinese friends—and by now she could be in serious trouble.'


Chang rapped three times on the cellar flagstones, the trapdoor opened and he climbed down into the darkness. Leela watched, fascinated, from her hiding place near the cellar door. She felt her impulse to jump on to the cab had been justified, since she had been able to track the enemy to his lair. Blissfully unaware that the Doctor already knew about the cellar hideout, Leela settled down to wait, with all the patience of a hunter outside the den of some dangerous wild beast.

In the secret chamber, Chang was bowing his head beneath the fury of his lord. Greel was occupied in hacking the carcase of a sheep into bloody chunks of raw meat. Chang winced as the cleaver thudded down. Such was Greel's fury that Chang felt his own neck might be the cleaver's next target. 'I will not tolerate failure,' roared Greel.

'There has been no failure, Lord.'

'Then where is the cabinet?'

Chang did not dare to confess that he had tried to obtain the Time Cabinet, and failed. Instead he told Greel that he had deliberately chosen to wait for a better opportunity, 'The house is marked and watched, Lord. When night returns, your servants of the Tong will descend and take the cabinet.'

'I put no trust in your opium-ridden scum,' snarled Greel. He gathered the chunks of raw meat into a pile and carried them across the chamber, dropping them in a heap by the far wall. Greel pulled a lever and a section of wall drew back to reveal a barred gap, beyond which was the dank blackness of a sewer tunnel. One by one Greel tossed the chunks of meat through the bars. He struck the gong that hung nearby, and a low booming note echoed through the cellar. Chang made another attempt to placate his Master. 'I promise, Lord, you shall have the Cabinet of Weng Chiang before the next sunset!'

Greel thrust a last chunk of meat between the bars. 'Do not fail me, Li H'sen Chang. I grow weary of this hole in the ground.'

'You are safe, here, Lord.'

'Safe?' The word only increased Greel's fury. 'This place is a trap, Chang. I was seen tonight as I returned.' He told Chang of his encounter with the Doctor.

There came a trumpeting squeal and a giant grey shape thudded against the bars. Huge teeth snapped down on the chunks of meat, dragging them away one by one. Greel gave a gloating laugh. 'My little pets, Li H'sen. My offerings have made them larger and more savage than any lion. None may attack us through the sewers while my pets stand guard!'

From the blackness behind the bars came savage grunts as the giant rat devoured the meat. Greel listened with satisfaction. It had amused him to feed the rats on the specially treated meat, irradiated in a way that caused them to grow to enormous size. He had little enough amusement, living like a rat himself in this hole in the ground.

Turning away from the bars, Greel returned to his grievance. 'Yes, Chang, the Doctor almost captured me. And he was led here by *your* blundering!'

Chang's eyes glittered with rage and resentment. 'He shall die, Lord!'

'The list of your failures is growing,' hissed Greel malevolently. He brooded for a moment. 'When you do succeed in obtaining the Time Cabinet, I must be ready to move quickly. I shall need strength.'

'I will bring a girl, Lord.'

'Two girls, Chang. I need *two* strong young donors, and I need them *now*.'

Chang remembered his earlier promise. But then he had had the whole night before him. It was too difficult to snatch up any girl unwary enough to be out so late. Now it was morning, and the streets would be full of the City's peasants whose work started early. Dock workers, factory girls, cleaning women ... There would be people everywhere—and the accursed police for ever on the watch. It was the nature of his god to be demanding. But no servant, however faithful, could achieve the impossible. 'It will be dangerous, Lord. The streets at this hour are busy...'

Greel's long-taloned hands seized him by the throat in a choking grip, shook him savagely and hurled him across the cellar to the foot of the ladder. 'No excuse. Get them!'

Chang picked himself up, his heart filled with resentment that he dared not show. 'Yes, Lord,' he said submissively, and turned to climb the ladder.

Leela ducked back into hiding as the trapdoor opened and Chang climbed through the gap. The door closed behind him, and he went up the cellar stairs. Leela slipped silently after him.

Still in pyjamas and dressing-gown, Professor Litefoot came yawning and stretching into the dining-room, and found the Doctor sitting at the dining-room table, drawing a map on the cloth with a silver pencil.

Litefoot looked at his strange guest in astonishment. 'Haven't you even slept, Doctor?'

'Sleep is for tortoises,' said the Doctor severely, and went on drawing his map.

'Miss Leela hasn't returned then?'

'Not yet.'

'Perhaps we should inform the police?'

'With nine missing girls on their list already, they won't have much time to spare for a tenth. But tell them by all means—and ask them to put a police guard on the house.'

'Surely those other poor girls disappeared in different circumstances?'

'Unless I manage to rescue her, Leela may well suffer exactly the same fate. I think I know why those girls were taken.' The Doctor leaped to his feet and paced angrily about the room. 'Some slavering, gangrenous vampire comes out of the sewers and stalks this city at night. I shall attack him in his lair!'

Litefoot peered at the map on the table-cloth. 'What's all this about?'

'I've been trying to work out an approach through the sewers.' The Doctor pointed to the map. 'Here's the Thames. This is the course of the River Fleet. And this is the Palace Theatre.'

'How do you know the course of the Fleet? It's been covered for centuries.'

The Doctor smiled reminiscently. 'I caught a salmon there once that would have hung over the sides of this table. Shared it with the Venerable Bede. He loved fish.'

Litefoot gave him a worried look, wondering if the

events of the night had affected the Doctor's brain. 'Do you need the map any more?'

The Doctor shook his head and Litefoot bundled up the cloth. 'I'd better dispose of this before my housekeeper sees it!' He took the cloth out of the room, dropping it into the laundry basket on the porch. When he returned, the Doctor was putting on his cape, and adjusting his deerstalker to a jaunty angle. 'Time we were off, Professor. Do you happen to have an elephant gun by any chance?'

'I've a Chinese fowling piece, if that's any good. Used for duck mainly. It's somewhere in the cellar.' Litefoot left the room for a few minutes and returned carrying a canvas bag, and a fearsome looking weapon, which he handed to the Doctor. It was an ancient long-barrelled muzzle-loader, a cross between a rifle and blunderbuss. 'I've even got the powder and shot for it here.' Litefoot tapped the canvas bag.

The Doctor took the heavy weapon and examined it. 'Splendid, Professor. Made in Birmingham, I see!' Opening the bag he started to load the weapon. 'Do you know where we can hire a small boat?'

'I imagine so.' Litefoot was beginning to wonder what extraordinary request the Doctor would come up with next. 'May I ask the purpose of these preparations?'

'First we shall find the confluence of the Thames and the Fleet, Professor. Then I shall follow the Fleet upstream to a point close to the villain's lair!' The Doctor aimed the enormous gun through the window and looked menacingly along the barrel. 'And then, Professor, we shall see what we shall see!'

# 8

## The Sacrifice

Leela trailed Chang through the maze of little back streets around the theatre. For quite some time, she followed him at a safe distance, constantly ducking out of sight round corners or behind garden walls. Luckily for her Chang seemed to have no suspicion that he might be followed. He wandered about almost aimlessly, with an air of worried preoccupation.

In fact, Chang was obsessed with carrying out his master's almost impossible command. Conditions could scarcely have been worse. At this hour the streets were almost deserted. Very soon they would be all too busy. Chang's usual hunting time was the hours after midnight, when there was a chance of picking up some solitary girl whose absence would go unnoticed, at least for a time. Where was he to find *two* suitable girls, so soon after dawn?

He was lurking at the mouth of a secluded cul-de-sac when a hansom-cab drove along the street and stopped outside one of the little houses. A girl in cloak and bonnet got out and paid off the driver, and the cab rattled away. Purposefully Chang stalked onward, unaware that Leela was close behind him.

Teresa Hart was a waitress in a gambling club, in Mayfair on the other side of London. Play usually went on until the small hours of the morning, and she often got home to bed at a time when others were getting up. She was fumbling for her key when a shadow fell over her doorway, and a voice said, 'Pleasant are the dreams of morning.'

She whirled round to find Chang bowing at her.
'You gave me a turn, dearie!'

'Fresh as dew and bright with promise,' said Chang with another bow.

Teresa sighed. She was quite used to being approached by strange gentlemen, particularly those who'd been out for a night on the town. She smiled and shook her head. 'All I want is a pair of kippers, a cup of tea and a bit of kip.'

'Budding lotus of the dawn, Chang has other plans for you.'

'Well, I can tell you what to do with them,' began Teresa spiritedly. Then she broke off. The stranger's eyes seemed to be burning, turning into glowing points of light.

'You will come with me,' said Chang. Teresa followed him.

Leela followed them both back to the theatre, and saw Chang take Teresa into his dressing-room. 'Await my return,' he ordered and went out into the corridor.

From her hiding place, Leela saw Chang pause irresolutely. A burst of laughter came from the auditorium—*female* laughter. As Chang made his way on to the stage, Leela slipped into the dressing-room.

The girl was sitting on a chair staring blankly into space. When Leela passed a hand in front of her face she didn't even blink. Clearly she was under an evil spell. Leela looked round the room, and saw the tall wardrobe cupboard where Chang kept his costumes. She opened it, and looked back at the hypnotised girl. A plan was forming in her mind . . .

Chang peered through a gap in the stage curtain, and saw a band of chattering cleaning women working busily in the otherwise empty theatre, sweeping and dusting between the rows of seats. Most were middle-aged, but a younger one was sweeping the orchestra pit below him. Swiftly Chang dropped down into the pit. The girl looked up opening her mouth to scream. But Chang's eyes burned into hers, and she shut her mouth and stood still. 'Come,' whispered Chang, and the girl followed him out of the pit.

Exultant with success, Chang hurried into his dressing-room. A female figure, head bowed and face obscured by a bonnet, sat waiting in the chair.

Leela waited breathlessly, wondering if her masquerade would be discovered. As she'd hoped, Chang scarcely bothered to look at her. Then to her horror she saw that the wardrobe door was swinging open, revealing Teresa in her petticoat propped inside. But Chang was too impatient to notice. Seizing Leela by the wrist he dragged her into the corridor, where the cleaning girl stood waiting.

Chang bustled the two girls towards the cellar steps. 'Hurry,' he hissed. 'My master must be fed!'


Early morning mist drifted over the river, and a cargo steamer gave a mournful hoot as it prepared to cast off. The old boatman sculled his boat along the bank of the river, wondering about his two strange passengers. The taller of them had an enormous fowling piece balanced across his knees. Where did he think he was, the Norfolk marshes? Someone should tell him London docks was no place for duck shooting. The waterman chewed meditatively on his quid of tobacco, and spat over the side into the Thames. After all, it was none of his business. He'd been handsomely paid, that was all he was worried about.

The Doctor smiled quietly to himself, guessing at the thoughts in the old man's mind. He wondered what the man would think if he knew what they were really hunting.

As they rowed along, the Doctor's keen eyes were constantly scanning the river bank. Suddenly he stood up, making the boat rock dangerously. 'There it is— that creek inlet over there!'

'Do sit down, Doctor,' said Litefoot peevishly. 'I assure you the boatman knows his business.'

The Doctor sat down. 'I always enjoyed messing about in boats!' As usual, the approach of danger found him in tremendous spirits. Litefoot frowned disapprovingly. 'I must say, Doctor, I think this entire enterprise is extremely rash.'

'My dear Litefoot, thanks to your invaluable help, I have a lantern, an excellent pair of waders and probably the most fearsome piece of hand artillary in England. What can possibly go wrong?'

Litefoot looked dubiously at the ancient fowling piece. 'That thing can, for a start. With the amount of buckshot you crammed in there, it'll probably explode in your face.'

'Unthinkable,' said the Doctor solemnly. 'You forget, it was made in England.'

Stolidly the boatman rowed towards the inlet.


Greel was busy at the controls of the machine that filled one corner of his underground chamber. There was a hum of power, and the central cabinet began to glow with life. Greel turned from his instruments and studied the waiting victims. 'Where did you get these girls?' he croaked irritably. He pinched Leela's arm, then moved to the second girl.

'Are they unsuitable, Lord?'

Greel examined the cleaning girl's arm. 'This one

has muscles like a horse,' he grumbled. 'Oh, I suppose they'll do. At least they're young, their life essence is still strong.'

'They are but peasant wenches, Lord. I took what I could find. It was not easy ...'

Irritably Greel waved him aside. 'Why must you always whine and complain so, Chang? I have given you knowledge that makes you a ruler among your fellows. And what do I ask in return? A few pitiful slatterns who will never be missed.'

'But they *are* missed, Lord,' said Chang. Greel seemed to have no understanding of the terrible risks he was taking. 'Because of your urgent need I was forced to act rashly. One of these girls I took from the theatre above us. Nobody saw. But when she is missed, it will bring the police ever nearer.'

Greel turned away. 'It is of no consequence. Once I have the Time Cabinet I shall leave here.' He thrust the cleaning girl towards Chang. 'Put this one in the dilation chamber, then go. Leave me to my work.'

As Chang led the girl to the machine, Greel glanced at Leela. 'Stay here. I shall not keep you waiting long.' He turned back to his instruments.


The Doctor climbed out of the boat and into the tunnel-like opening of the sewer outlet. Litefoot passed him the gun and the lantern. 'All right, Doctor?'

'All right, Professor.' The Doctor produced a match, and lit his lantern.

Litefoot hesitated. 'I'll wait for you here then?'

'That's right,' said the Doctor cheerfully. 'If I'm still in here at high tide—don't bother to wait any longer.'

'Good luck, then, Doctor.'

'Thank you,' said the Doctor. Gun in one hand,

lantern in the other, he disappeared into the darkness of the tunnel.


Leela stood in the corner of Greel's chamber considering her next move. For the moment she was forgotten. Chang had left the cellar, and the strange black-masked being was busy with the victim now in the machine. Leela knew she must act soon if she was to rescue her fellow captive.

Greel fixed the girl in the cabinet, adjusting the two metal spheres so that they rested one each side of her head. He stepped back and looked at her, nodding in satisfaction. 'A few minor readjustments and all will be ready,' he muttered. Once more he bent over the controls.

Leela slipped quietly out of Teresa's dress. The garments hampered her movements, and soon she would be fighting for her life. Stepping out of the dress she stood in camisole and long Victorian pantaloons. Not so practical as the animal-skin costume she wore on her native planet, but it would have to do. She saw that Greel had completed his adjustments, and was standing back for a final check. Leela crept silently towards him and as Greel reached for the master-lever, she sprang.

She was a fraction late, and Greel had time to wrench back the lever before he went down under her attack. There was a fierce hum of power, the machine vibrated and lightning arced between the two metal spheres, passing through the head of the unfortunate cleaning girl. She went rigid, her mouth opening in a silent scream. Gradually her skin began to wither.

Leela and Greel rolled over and over, fighting furiously, and dropped into the culvert that ran down the side of the chamber. Leela landed on top, and gripping Greel by the throat she began throttling him with all her strength. Greel's body went suddenly limp. Leela let go of the scrawny neck, climbed out of the culvert and ran over to the machine. To her horror she saw the body of the cleaning girl had turned into a mummified husk. Leela tried frantically to switch off the machine, but could make nothing of the maze of controls in front of her. The machine gave a final surge of power and the cleaning girl's body disappeared. The vibrating died down, and the machine seemed to switch itself off, the grisly process complete. A retort-like container connected to the machine glowed brightly, as it filled with some luminous fluid.

Leela realised that all she could do now was to save herself. She climbed the ladder, but the opening to the cellar was closed. Clinging to the top of the ladder Leela began heaving desperately at the trapdoor.

Below her, Greel stirred, and crept feebly from the culvert. He crawled painfully across the floor and pulled himself upright, snatching a laser-pistol from a bench.

Leela felt a blast of heat and a chunk of stonework beside her head exploded into dust. She dropped cat-like from the ladder and rolled over between the benches for shelter, dropping into the culvert where she had fought with Greel.

There was another blast, and a piece of the wall beside her was blown away. Leela could see only one chance of escape. Hurling the nearest container at Greel's head to distract his aim, she squeezed through the gap below the bars at the end of the culvert. Wriggling through she dropped into the darkness of the sewer tunnel, just as another shot blasted the stonework. She scrambled to her feet and flattened herself into a niche in the tunnel wall, and waited panting.

In the chamber, Greel moved to follow her through

the culvert, then drew back. The girl had been terrifyingly strong, and even with the laser-pistol he would be at a disadvantage in the darkness. An evil smile twisted the distorted lips beneath Greel's leather mask. There was a better way.

He hobbled to the lever that controlled his feeding-hatch and pulled it. The hatch slid open. Snatching up his hammer Greel beat again and again on the gong. The booming notes echoed away down the tunnel. The sound would bring the giant rats scuttling for their meat. But this time there would be no meat. Only Leela.

Greel gave a maniacal laugh. 'When my beauties find her,' he snarled, 'she will wish she had died here in my machine.'

From somewhere in the sewer tunnel came the hungry squeal of a giant rat.

# 9

## In the Jaws of the Rat

Leela stood waiting silently for a moment, the sound of the gong ringing in her ears. As it faded she heard an angry squealing. She hurried along the sewer tunnel away from the terrifying sound.

Lantern held high, the Doctor splashed through the murky stream that flowed down the centre of the sewer. He came to a T-junction and paused to review his mental picture of the map he had drawn on Litefoot's table-cloth. Taking the left turn he splashed steadily on his way. If his calculations were correct, the cellar hideout was very near.

Sitting in the rowing boat just outside the sewer outlet, Professor Litefoot looked at his watch for the tenth time. The tide would be rising soon. The Doctor's time was almost up. Litefoot sighed, and put another match to his pipe. He tossed the spent match into the river, and watched it float away. Hunched over his oars, the boatman spat impassively into the water.

Meanwhile a brightly painted horse-drawn cart was drawing up outside Professor Litefoot's door. A policeman stepped suspiciously out of the shrubbery. 'Here, what's all this?'

The pig-tailed Chinese driver appeared to speak no

English. He chatted incomprehensibly, and pointed to the side of the cart, on which was written, 'LIMEHOUSE LAUNDRY CO.' He pointed to the porch where there stood a wicker hamper, the same words written on the label on its side. He opened the back of his cart, and pointed to an identical hamper, making crossover gestures with his hands.

The constable grinned. 'I get you, Johnny. Clean laundry come, dirty washing go away!'

The Chinese bowed and smiled. He took the basket from his van, and put it on the porch, lifted the basket on the porch into the back of his van. Jumping into the driving seat, he cracked his whip and drove away.

Wondering vaguely why the Chinese had such an affinity with laundries, the constable resumed his patrol around the house. As he moved away, the lid of the wicker basket moved slightly, and then became still. Now there was a tiny gap between basket and lid— just big enough for someone to look out.

Arriving at the theatre to start his day's work, Casey was scandalised to see a half-dressed female run out of Chang's dressing-room. 'Hey, you,' he called. 'What do you think you're doing?'

The girl stared blankly at him. 'Where am I? What happened to me last night? I can't remember.'

Casey grabbed her by the arm. 'I'll remember *you* all right if anything's missing.'

Indignantly Teresa pulled away. 'You keep your hands off me, I'm a lady,' she screamed.

Jago came on the scene, to find a fine old shouting match going on. 'Now then, Casey, what's the trouble?'

'No trouble, Mr Jago, sir. Just seeing this lady off the premises.'

Jago turned sternly to Teresa, but she ignored him.

She was staring in terror at a poster on the wall—the poster that bore Chang's face. 'It was him,' she gasped. 'Oh my lord, it was him! Let me out of this place!' She turned and ran out of the still-open stage door.

Jago said thoughtfully, 'Remember this incident, Casey. It may have some relevance to the investigation.'

'What's that, sir?'

'The investigation, Casey,' whispered Jago mysteriously. 'Last night I made the acquaintance of a very high-up gentleman, an amateur investigator called in by Scotland Yard.' Jago's chest swelled with pride. '*I* am assisting him, Casey!'

Casey's eyes widened. 'No!'

'I am. He has asked me to watch, Casey. And I am watching—everywhere!' Jago disappeared into his office. Casey shrugged wonderingly, and disappeared backstage. After a moment Chang stepped from the doorway where he had been watching and hurried towards the cellar steps.

The moment he entered Greel's chamber a storm of rage broke over his head. 'Fool,' screamed Greel. 'Stupid incompetent fool!' Angrily he told of Leela's attack on him, and of her escape into the sewers. 'She was a tigress. Had I not feigned death, she would have killed me!'

'I can explain, Lord,' pleaded Chang. 'She substituted herself for the girl I had chosen. And I recognise your description of her. She was with the Doctor.'

Greel hobbled to a metal chair close to his extraction machine, and fastened electrodes to his wasted body. He operated controls and the retort glowed brightly and then faded again. There was a rushing sound as the life essence of the sacrificed girl flooded into Greel's body. Greel waited for a moment, then stood up. As he removed the electrodes he could feel the strength returning to his body. But he knew all too well that the effect was only temporary. Soon he would weaken again, and it would need more donors, and yet more, to keep him from wasting away. The knowledge added to his anger, and he turned once more on the unhappy Chang.

'You have failed me, Li H'sen. You know that until I have the Time Cabinet I can never be whole, never be cured of this wasting sickness...'

'Lord, hear me,' pleaded Chang. 'I would lay down my life in your service. You shall have the Time Cabinet tonight, the plans are already made...'

'Fail me once more and I shall dismiss you, Chang. I cannot leave my fate in such blundering hands.'

Chang fell to his knees. 'Great One, I shall find this Doctor. I shall strike him down for the harm he has done you!'

Greel waved him away. 'Do not beg, unworthy one. Go!'


Leela ran frantically through the sewers. From somewhere behind her came the savage squealing of the giant rats. Summoned by the gong, they had come rushing to Greel's feeding hatch. Leela had managed to dodge them, hiding in an alcove as the great grey shapes came rushing by. Finding no meat at the grating the monsters had begun casting about the tunnels.

Leela ran blindly on. Since she had no idea where she was or where she was heading she was as likely to run into one of the creatures as to escape from them. Her only hope was to keep on the move.

Suddenly she heard a fierce trumpeting squeal close behind her. One of the monsters had picked up her scent.

Not far away, the Doctor heard the squeal. He paused to check his fowling piece, then moved towards the sound.

Leela sped on through the darkness. She could hear scurrying footsteps behind her, and the angry screams of the giant rat. She tripped and fell, and struggled desperately to her feet again. Wet and filthy now, she staggered on. A tiny point of light appeared in the tunnel far ahead. With the last of her failing strength, she reeled towards it.

The Doctor heard the terrifying roar of the giant rat. Calmly he placed his lantern on a ledge and raised the gun to his shoulder.

A shape loomed up, the Doctor sighted along the barrel of the gun ... and realised that the shape was Leela!

Hastily lowering the gun, he called, 'Leela, it's me!'

Leela paused for a moment, gasping with relief—and the giant rat sprang out of the darkness and seized her leg. She gave a despairing scream, as the rat began dragging her back along the tunnel.

# 10

# A Plan to Kill the Doctor

For an agonised moment the Doctor hesitated. To shoot with the rat and Leela so close together meant taking a terrible risk. But there was no alternative. He dropped to one knee, threw the gun to his shoulder, aimed and fired.

There was a great boom of an explosion, and the recoil of the heavy weapon made him stagger back. Clouds of black smoke poured from the barrel of the gun, and peering through the haze, the Doctor saw Leela crawling towards him. Behind her the giant rat lay on its side, a gaping hole in its chest, lips drawn back from the yellow fangs in a dying snarl.

The Doctor helped Leela to rise. 'Are you all right?'

Leela rubbed her leg. 'I think so—the teeth just bruised me. Some use in these stupid clothes after all.'

'You were lucky.'

'I deserve to die, Doctor. I had the chance to kill our enemy, and I failed.'

The Doctor took off his cape and wrapped it round Leela's shoulders. 'What chance? Where?'

A distant roar came echoing down the tunnel. The Doctor picked up his gun. 'The trouble with this thing is it takes about half an hour to load. Come on, Leela. You can tell me what you've been up to on the way back.'

With preparations for the evening meal well under way, Jago decided to slip out to the pub across the street for a little liquid refreshment. He was just leaving the theatre by the stage door when he met Li H'sen Chang, who was just arriving. 'Here already, Mr Chang?' said Jago jovially. 'I shall have to start charging you rent for that dressing-room.'

Chang smiled coldly. 'There is much to prepare before the performance, Mr Jago.'

'Yes, of course, of course. The art that conceals art, eh? Tell me, Mr Chang ...' Jago paused awkwardly. 'About last night...'

'Yes?'

'Think I must be working too hard, overcrowding the old brainbox. I know I spoke to you about your contract, but I've forgotten how we left matters...'

'I am considering your new offer.'

'Ah, I see. A generous offer, was it, Mr Chang?'

'Merely—reasonable.' Chang turned to go to his dressing-room, then paused. 'Incidentally, I shall be appearing tonight without Mr Sin. He is—indisposed.'

Jago chuckled. 'Very droll. I shall treasure that witticism, Mr Chang. Indisposed, eh? I suppose the poor little fellow's got a touch of woodworm, eh?'

Ignoring Jago's little joke, Chang turned and headed for the dressing-room. Jago mopped his brow and plunged through the stage door. Somehow after his meeting with Chang, he needed a drink more than ever.


The Doctor was sitting wrong way round on one of Litefoot's dining-room chairs, folded arms resting on the high back, chin resting on his arms. He was staring fixedly at the Time Cabinet, as if hoping to fathom its secrets by sheer will power. Leela was warming her hands at the blazing fire, still swathed in the Doctor's cape. She was telling him about the girl who had been sacrificed in Greel's machine.

'She aged and withered, Doctor. Her skin went dry, like old leaves. The machine did it to her. Then she vanished...'

'Dry, like old leaves,' repeated the Doctor thoughtfully. 'It sounds like organic distillation. Her life-essence was drained away.'

'Why? What is our enemy doing?'

The Doctor jumped up. 'He doesn't *know* what he's doing,' he shouted in sudden anger. 'He's a madman. A monstrously deranged sociopath!'

The door opened and Litefoot staggered in. He was loaded down with parcels, which he passed over to Leela with a sigh of relief. 'There's your new outfit, my dear. I hope it's suitable. If you'd like to take these things upstairs Mrs Hudson will help you change.'

Leela went out with the parcels, and Litefoot sank into a chair, mopping his brow. 'Dashed embarrassing business, that, choosing togs for a young lady. You have to be jolly careful it's the right fashion. Clothes matter to women.'

'They do?' said the Doctor abstractedly. He resumed his study of the Time Cabinet, running his hands over the surface. There was a saucer-shaped depression in the middle of what was presumably the door. 'A keyhole,' muttered the Doctor. 'But where's the key?'

'Still trying to get that thing open, Doctor?'

'I'm trying to place the exact period. It can only be opened by a key of the correct molecular combination.'

'Heard you shouting as I opened the front door. Something about a madman...'

'Yes. Weng-Chiang. He's probably got the key.'

'Weng-Chiang? He was one of the ancient Chinese gods.'

'This Weng-Chiang's no god. He must have arrived in your Time Zone in this contraption.' The Doctor tapped the cabinet. 'What do you know of its history?'

'It was a gift to Mama from His Highness, T'ungchi. Been in the family for years.'

'You're lucky he hasn't traced it before now,' said the Doctor broodingly.

Leela came back resplendent in a new gown.

'Charming,' said Litefoot immediately. 'Don't you think so, Doctor?'

The Doctor focused his attention on Leela. 'What? Oh yes, quite delightful. I shall be proud to escort you to the Palace Theatre tonight.'

Leela was pleased in spite of herself. The clothes of this century were ridiculous and impractical—but they were rather becoming in their way. 'Then we're going to the theatre after all, Doctor?'

'That's right. We've an appointment with the great Li H'sen Chang.' The Doctor beamed, cheered up as always by the prospect of action. 'Tell you what, Leela. If you're a very good girl—I might even buy you an orange!'

Jago stood backstage, watching the bustle of activity all around him. The first House had gone off well, and now it was almost time for the second to begin. As always, once the performance got under way, the evening seemed to flash by at an incredible pace.

He went on to the stage itself, and peered through the gap in the curtains. The house was filling up nicely —though disappointingly there was still no sign of the one person he'd most hoped to see.

'Looking for someone, Mr Jago?' said a familiar voice behind him.

Jago turned. 'The Doctor, Casey. My collaborator

and fellow-sleuth. No sign of him yet. Oh well, he'll be here, Casey. I'll lay a guinea to a gooseberry on it!'

Behind them, in the centre of the stage, Chang was checking the operation of a trap-door that was used in his act. He straightened up at Jago's words, and went to his dressing-room. He took a shining nickel-plated revolver from a drawer and began to load it. If the Doctor did come tonight, Chang would be waiting.

There was the sound of horses' hooves in the road outside, and Litefoot went to the window. 'There you are, Doctor, your cab's arrived.'

The Doctor was putting on his cape, and Litefoot turned to help Leela with her cloak. 'You'll need to wrap up. Fog's getting thick again.'

The Doctor paused at the door. 'I know there's a policeman outside, Professor, but don't just rely on him. Lock and bar your doors, as soon as we've gone— and keep your revolver handy.'

Litefoot saw them into the hall. 'You really think those scoundrels may return?'

'That Cabinet is vitally important to their master. They'll stop at nothing to get their hands on it. So be on your guard, Professor.'

'Don't worry, Doctor, I'll be ready for them. They won't catch George Litefoot napping a second time!'

Litefoot opened the front door and watched Leela and the Doctor get into the waiting cab. The driver cracked his whip, the cab rattled away and the patrolling policeman touched his helmet in salute, as it disappeared into the fog.

Litefoot noticed the laundry basket on the porch and thought vaguely that the laundry had delivered a day early. He dragged the hamper through the front

84

door and left it in the hall. Mrs Hudson would see to it in the morning. Returning to the sitting-room, Litefoot put some more coal on the fire and poured himself a large whisky and soda. Glass in one hand, revolver in the other, he settled down for his night's vigil.

Greel was busy dismantling his distillation machine. He paid no attention to Chang, who stood bowing low before him.

Unable to believe that his god would really desert him, Chang said, 'Lord, if this infidel Doctor does come here tonight, then I swear I shall kill him.'

Greel gave a mirthless laugh. 'It is far more likely that he will kill you.'

'No, Lord, I have made a plan to kill the Doctor in public, as a sacrifice to appease your wrath. To prove that I, above all others, am your true servant.'

Greel waved him away. 'You are unworthy to serve me, Li H'sen Chang. I shall lead the Tong myself, and take my own measures to recover the Time Cabinet. Now go!'

Chang bowed low, and turned to the ladder, more determined than ever to carry out his plan. Surely his god would forgive him ... once the Doctor was dead.

The second house was just about to start, and Jago was still scanning the audience. 'There he is, Casey. Look!'

Jago pointed upwards. Leela and the Doctor were just entering the 'Royal' box, the one just beside the stage. 'Trust him to take the best seats in the house,' said Jago admiringly.

Casey stared at the Doctor's tall figure. 'Doesn't look much like a detective to me.'

'Well, he's not going to wear a bowler hat and big boots, is he? High-up secret investigator, he is, a man of a thousand faces.'

'Who's the girl?'

'Window-dressing. Part of his disguise.' Jago turned away from the curtain. 'Think I'll just pop along and let him know we're standing by down here.' Jago's mind returned abruptly to the business of everyday life. 'Now then Casey, have you got that trap-door ready?'

'Not yet, Mr Jago, sir.'

'Then you'd better see to it, my lad—unless you want Mr Chang after you, for ruining his act.' Jago hurried away.

Casey called after him. 'The thing is, Mr Jago, it means going down into that cellar . . .'

But Jago was gone. Casey sighed, and moved slowly towards the cellar steps.


The Doctor and Leela were installed in their comfortable box. Leelt gazed round the fast-filling theatre with keen interest. Although she didn't really know what was going on, her keen senses were already picking up vibrations of pleasure and excitement in the air. It reminded her of the tribal festivals of her own people.

The Doctor was glancing through the programme when he heard a low 'Psst!' from somewhere near the floor. He looked down and saw Jago crawling into the box on his hands and knees. The Doctor smiled. 'Good evening, Mr Jago.'

'A pleasure to welcome you to my theatre, Doctor— and your charming companion.'

'Thank you. Are you quite comfortable down there?'

'I know the value of discretion, Doctor. May I ask if you've made any further deductions?'

'Quite a few, Mr Jago, quite a few.'

'I thought as much. No doubt you're on the point of solving the mystery of the missing maidens?'

'I expect further developments shortly,' said the Doctor mysteriously.

Jago was thrilled with the romance and excitement of it all. 'Well, if you need any help, I hope I know where my duty lies.'

The Doctor reached down and patted him on the shoulder. 'You're a brave man, Mr Jago. I knew I could count on you.'

'Still, I don't suppose you'll actually be needing me,' added Jago hastily. 'I expect you've got the place surrounded, eh? Armed men scattered in the audience?'

The Doctor shook his head.

Jago paled. 'You mean there's nobody?'

'Nobody,' said the Doctor solemnly. 'When the moments of danger comes, Mr Jago, you and I will face our destiny, shoulder to shoulder.'

'Oh, corks,' said Jago faintly, and backed slowly out of the box.

In fear and trembling, and working as fast as he could, Casey finished preparing the mechanism of the trap-door that formed part of Chang's act. His task completed, he was hurrying from the gloomy cellar when he heard a grinding sound from the corner arch. Terrified, Casey spun round. A black-cloaked figure was climbing up through the trap-door in the floor. It wore a loose-brimmed black hat, its fact was entirely covered in a black-leather mask and, incongruously, it was carrying a carpet-bag.

Casey made a terrified dart for the cellar stairs, but the apparition saw him. Dropping the bag it bounded after him with a terrifying snarl. Casey's foot slipped on the bottom stair, he fell and the apparition was upon him. As its skinny hands reached out, Casey heard faint sounds of music from the stage above. Then everything was drowned out by the frightened pounding of his heart ...

# 11

# Death on Stage

The soprano concluded her patriotic song, and exited to enthusiastic applause. The curtains were drawn and Jago appeared in front of them. 'And now, Ladies and gentlemen, it is my privilege to introduce to you, in his extended season here at the Palace, in the second of two appearances here this evening, someone whose legendary legerdemain has entertained all the crowned heads of Europe. Here to baffle and bewilder you, the world's foremost magician, straight from the mysterious Orient—ladies and gentlemen, Li H'sen Chang!'

The curtains drew back to reveal a painted backdrop intended to represent an oriental palace. Jago pointed dramatically to the centre of the empty stage and stepped hastily back. There was a brilliant flash, a cloud of smoke, and suddenly Chang was there, bowing low in his Oriental robes. 'Humble Chang is most honoured at this kind reception.' He snapped his fingers and the Chinese assistant Lee carried on a table upon which rested a pack of cards and a nickel-plated revolver. 'First tlick velly simple,' announced Chang. During his act he often spoke in the pidgin English that Englishmen expected from the Chinese. He picked up the cards from the table. 'Will someone take cards please?' Chang walked across to the side of the stage until he stood directly looking up at the Doctor's box. 'You sir? Please catchee cards?'

He tossed the pack into the air and the Doctor caught it. Chang bowed. 'Kindly assist humble magician by finding ace of diamonds and holding up so everyone can see!'

The Doctor found the card and held it up to the audience.

Chang bowed his thanks. 'Ah, so! Now please to put card back in middle of pack, and hold whole pack up with finger and thumb.'

Once more the Doctor obeyed. Chang took the revolver from the table. 'Chang will now shoot magic bullet through ace of diamonds, without hitting other cards. Honourable gentleman will please remain very still.'

Chang levelled the revolver from the stage. The Doctor stood upright in the box, the cards held before his chest like a target.

Leela looked worriedly up at him. 'Doctor, be careful ...'

The Doctor smiled. He knew that Chang intended to try to kill him. But he also knew that the magician wouldn't do it too obviously. This was merely a preliminary challenge, a test of nerve. Deliberately the Doctor moved the pack of cards so it was directly over his left-hand heart.

There was an excited murmur from the crowd, and Chang held up a reproving hand. 'Please to be very still. I shot fifteen peasants trying to learn this trick!'

Slowly Chang raised the revolver and fired. The Doctor stood quite still, and Chang called, 'If most courageous gentleman will now look for ace of diamonds?'

The Doctor found the card and held it up. There was a neat hole drilled through the centre. The crowd gave a round of applause, and the Doctor looked down at Chang. 'Oh, very good! Anything else I can do?'

Chang bowed once more. 'If honourable gentleman will please bring cards down to stage, I have further interesting demonstration, requiring assistant with nerves of steel.'

The Doctor gave Leela a reassuring smile, and left the box. Meanwhile, Lee, Chang's assistant, was wheeling a metal cabinet on stage. Chang flung open the doors and rapped on the sides, demonstrating its solid construction. The Doctor appeared at the side of the stage and Chang beckoned him forward. 'Now I will ask eager volunteer to step into Cabinet of Death.'

Chang smiled as the Doctor moved slowly towards the cabinet. He was banking on the fact that, as with the card trick, the Doctor would be too proud to refuse a public challenge. Once inside the cabinet, the Doctor would be doomed. It was a simple enough trick. The 'victim', usually a chorus-girl, stepped inside the cabinet, which was then closed and locked. Once inside, she pressed a hidden catch and the trick floor of the cabinet slid back. The cabinet was positioned directly over a trap-door in the stage, and at a signal from Chang, Casey would operate the trap-door so that the girl could drop out of the cabinet and under the stage. Chang would then pass swords through the special slits in the side of the empty cabinet. A few minutes later, he would withdraw the swords and give another signal. The girl would come up through the trap-door, there would be a bang and a flash, Chang would open the door and she would step from the cabinet unharmed.

That was the way things *usually* went. This time Chang planned a very different ending. Once the Doctor was inside the cabinet, Chang would thrust the razor sharp swords through the slits—with the Doctor still inside. The Doctor wouldn't know how to find the secret catch—and even if he did, Chang had no intention of giving Casey the signal to open the trap-door. The Doctor would be executed publicly, in full sight of his friends. And no one would be more horrified than Chang at the tragic accident—caused of course by an unfortunate jamming of the equipment.

The Doctor was at the cabinet by now, and at a nod from Chang, Lee attempted to thrust him inside. The Doctor dodged, Lee stumbled, and suddenly found that *he* was inside the cabinet. Instantly the Doctor closed and locked the doors, and turning to the crowd he gave an exaggerated bow. A burst of laughter came from the crowd. Chang glowered, but soon regained control of himself. 'The bird has flown. Alas, it seems that one of us is yellow!'

The crowd greeted Chang's sally with another burst of laughter—and no one laughed louder than the Doctor. Chang realised that the Doctor had outwitted him. All he could do now was go on with the trick.

Chang stretched out his hand and a long sharp sword seemed to appear from thin air. 'Play close attention ladies and gentlemen.' He swished the sword in the air and thudded it point-down into the stage to demonstrate its sharpness. The thud was in reality a signal to Casey down below. It should have been followed by the faint rumble that meant the trap was open. Chang listened, but heard nothing. Anxiously he drew out the sword, and thudded it into the boards once more.

Below the stage, Greel heard the repeated signal. He had formed a grim plan of his own. He would seal his rejection of Chang by punishing him with a public loss of face—the most humiliating fate that any Chinese can suffer. He reached out and pulled the lever, and Lee tumbled through the trap-door. At the sight of Greel, he prostrated himself on the ground in terror.

'*You* will serve me, now,' croaked Greel. 'Now listen to my instructions. The sacred things in the secret chamber must be taken to the House of the Dragon, and the Time Cabinet recovered. Summon your brothers of the Tong to help you. Meanwhile *I* shall deal with our great magician ...'


Chang heard the faint vibration of the trap, and sure that the cabinet was empty, he continued with his act. Keeping up a steady stream of comic patter, he began passing sword after sword through the slits in the cabinet. 'In my country,' he hissed, 'this is known as the death of the thousand cuts.' When the last sword was in place, Chang bowed, and spun the cabinet round on its base to reveal that the swords had passed completely through.

He replaced the cabinet and began removing the swords. As he took the last one out he gestured to the Doctor. 'Now, if my new assistant will kindly open the cabinet?'

The Doctor threw open the cabinet door—and Casey fell out on to the stage. There was laughter from the crowd, which turned to uneasy murmuring as the huddled body did not move. A woman screamed ...

In the wings Jago grabbed his chief stagehand. 'Get that curtain down—quick!'

As the curtains began to close, Jago ran out in front of them and made a brief, incoherent announcement. 'Ladies and gentlemen ... unfortunate accident. No cause for alarm. Performance will continue shortly ...' He waved frantically at the conductor and the orchestra struck up a rousing tune.

Jago hurried backstage to find the Doctor kneeling by Casey's body. 'For heaven's sake, what happened, Doctor?'

'He's dead—died of fright. Poor chap must have had a weak heart.'

Leela ran on to the stage. 'What happened, Doctor? Did the magician kill him?'

The Doctor shook his head. 'No, Chang was as surprised as anyone.' He looked round. 'Incidentally—where's he got to?'

Despairing, Chang looked round Greel's now-empty secret chamber. The equipment, the distillation chamber, everything was gone. 'The great lord Weng-Chiang has deserted me,' sobbed Chang, and fell to his knees.

He was still kneeling, head bowed, when the Doctor and Leela came down the ladder. He looked up at them apathetically. 'It seems you've been left to carry the can, Chang,' said the Doctor.

Chang raised a hand to his mouth and the Doctor pounced, tugging the dragon-seal ring from his finger. 'No poison for you. There are questions to be answered.'

Chang got to his feet, struggling to recover his dignity. 'I will say nothing. It is time for me to rejoin my ancestors.'

'Tell me about Weng-Chiang,' insisted the Doctor. 'Where's he gone now?'

Chang looked vaguely at him. 'Back to his palace in the sky, perhaps. He was displeased with me ...'

'His mind is broken,' whispered Leela.

The Doctor stared hypnotically into Chang's dazed eyes, willing him to answer. 'You know he's not really a god, don't you? When did you meet?'

Chang's voice became a chant. 'He came like a god, in a glowing cabinet of fire. He came forth and collapsed, weakened by his journey. I was only a humble peasant, but I gave him sanctuary in my hut.'

'What about the Time Cabinet?'

'The soldiers of the Emperor came upon it by chance. They took it away, while my lord was still sick. When he began to recover we searched for it. We learned that it had been given as a gift to a foreign devil-woman who had left the shores of China. Ever since we have searched for the great Cabinet of Weng-Chiang. The god is still sick. He will not be whole until it is found.'

Jago clattered down the ladder and looked round the chamber in astonishment. 'Well, cover me in creosote, I never knew this was here. A cellar under the cellar!'

'Doctor, look out,' called Leela, but it was too late.

Taking advantage of the distraction, Chang ducked into the culvert through which Leela had once made her escape and disappeared into the sewers. Leela started to follow him, but the Doctor restrained her. 'No, Leela.'

'But he'll escape.'

'There's no escape that way. He's gone to join his ancestors.'

From somewhere in the sewers came the scream of a giant rat.


Chang was running frantically through the sewers when he heard the scream. It was somewhere in front of him, very close. He turned and began running towards the hidden chamber, but it was too late. A giant rat sprang out of the darkness, and bore him down. Its teeth closed on his leg, and it began dragging him back towards its lair.

Jago stared around him in fascination. 'So the Celestial Chang really was involved in these Machiavellian machinations?'

'Up to his epicanthic eyelids,' said the Doctor solemnly.

'Well I'll go to Australia!' said Jago. A scream from the sewer cut him short. 'What in the name of heaven ...'

The Doctor turned away. 'You'll need a new top of the bill, I'm afraid.'

'Chang?' whispered Jago.

The Doctor nodded. 'There are giant rats roaming those sewers, Mr Jago. You'd better warn the authorities to seal off this whole section. Cyanide gas will probably settle the brutes ...'

Searching for clues, Leela flung open a corner cabinet. 'Look, Doctor. Women's clothes, lots of them.'

'All that's left of the victims,' said the Doctor grimly.

Jago stared at him. 'The missing girls! So it was Chang?'

'Not Chang. His master—the monstrous crazed maniac who caused all this.'

Leela pointed to the empty corner. 'The death-machine has gone, Doctor.'

'Precisely. He plans to start all over again somewhere else. I've got to find him.'

'But he could be anywhere.' Leela looked at the pathetic bundle of clothes. 'Why did he destroy those girls?'

'He needed their life-essence to survive,' said the Doctor impatiently. 'Unfortunately, the more he absorbs, the more grossly deformed he becomes.'

Leela tried to translate all this into terms she could understand. 'You mean he is like a water-bag with a hole in it—pouring in more water only makes the hole grow bigger?'

The Doctor looked at her in mild surprise. 'That's exactly right—a very good analogy, Leela.'

'What made him like that?'

'An experiment that went wrong,' said the Doctor slowly. 'A dangerous experiment in time travel. It upset the balance of his metabolism. Now he's fighting to restore it by drawing on the life-force of others. Come on, Leela, we'd better get back to that Time Cabinet.' He climbed the ladder and Leela followed him.

Left on his own, Jago was struck by sudden inspiration. 'Got it,' he said. 'I'll run tours of inspection. See the lair of the phantom—a bob a nob!'


Litefoot's head nodded on to his chest, and he awoke with a sudden start. The coal fire in the grate had burned low. He must have been asleep for quite some time.

He got stiffly to his feet, went over to the window and drew back the curtain. In the circle of light cast by the lamp over the porch, he saw the patrolling policeman, stamping his feet to keep warm. Litefoot felt a pang of sympathy for the poor fellow out in the cold and fog. Reassured, he put some more coal on the fire and poked it into a blaze, then sank back into his comfortable chair.

Outside, the policeman yawned and stretched, and decided to take a turn around the house. Daft idea anyway, all this, he thought. What did old Professor Litefoot need guarding for?

Bored and sleepy, the policeman didn't notice the lithe black-clad figures slipping through the shrubbery and moving ever closer to the house. As he turned to begin his patrol, a hatchet spun out of the darkness and thudded into the back of his neck. He dropped without a sound, and the servants of the Tong began converging on the house.

In the hall, the lid of the laundry basket suddenly flew off. Mr Sin sat upright, eyes wide open, knife in hand.

# 12

# The Hunt for Greel

The Doctor paid off the cab driver, who raised his whip in salute and drove away. Leela made straight for Litefoot's front door, but the Doctor put a hand on her arm. 'Wait.'

'What's the matter?'

The Doctor pointed. 'Over there.' A booted foot was projecting from a clump of shrubbery. They went over and found the body of the constable, thrust carelessly out of sight.

Leela whirled to face the house. 'Our enemies are here!'

'I doubt it. They've probably been and gone.'

They went to the front door, and found it slightly ajar. The Doctor pointed to the array of locks and bolts on the inside. 'No sign of forced entry. Someone let them in.'

They found Litefoot sprawled on the floor of the sitting-room, blood trickling from an ugly bruise on his forehead.

Leela pointed. 'The Time Cabinet, Doctor. It's gone!'

The pigtailed driver cracked his whip and the black carriage rattled over the cobbles. The Time Cabinet was strapped on the roof. Inside the carriage sat Greel, Mr Sin lolling beside him. Greel's wasted body was shaking with maniacal laughter.

Litefoot could tell them little when he revived. He had been dozing in his chair, the door had been flung open and a horde of black-clad figures had overwhelmed him.

'Chinese Tong-wallahs,' said Litefoot indignantly. 'Funny thing is, I didn't hear 'em breaking in.'

The Doctor was standing in the doorway, looking at the laundry basket in the hall. 'Was one of them a midget, by any chance?'

'That's right. How the devil did you know?'

'Elementary, my dear Litefoot. He arrived in your laundry basket, and let the others in.'

Leela went on bathing Litefoot's forehead. 'That creature was here before, Doctor. I fought with it in this room.'

'That's right.' The Doctor sank wearily into an armchair. 'I've worked out what all this is about, now. Everything fits. Chang's Mr Sin is really the Peking Homunculus. It was made in Peking, and presented as a gift to the Commissioner of the Icelandic Alliance, somewhere around the year five thousand.'

'Preposterous!' snorted Litefoot.

Leela waved him to silence. It wasn't often the Doctor was in the mood to explain anything. 'Sssh! Go on, Doctor!'

The Doctor told a horrifying story of war and carnage in the far-distant future. Much of it Leela and the Professor found hard to follow. Somehow it was all tied up with the sinister little manikin. 'It was supposed to be a toy, a plaything for the Commissioner's children. It was operated by a series of magnetic circuits and a small computer, with one organic component—the cerebral cortex of a pig.'

The Doctor paused, remembering the future. 'In reality it was an assassination weapon. It massacred

100

the Commissioner and all his family. That's what set off World War Six. Somehow the thing has been brought from that age to this.'

Litefoot poured himself a large brandy. ''Pon my soul, Doctor, this is a dashed queer story. Time travel, eh?'

'Unsuccessful time travel, Professor. Findecker's discovery of the double nexus particle sent human science of that era into a technological cul-de-sac.'

'Ah,' said Litefoot wisely. To Leela he whispered, 'Are you following any of this?'

'Not a word!'

Unaware that he had left his audience far behind him, the Doctor went on. 'Clearly this pig-thing is still alive. It needs a human operator of course, but the mental feedback is so intense the swinish instinct becomes dominant. It hates humanity, and revels in carnage . . .'

Leela decided she'd had all the explanation she could handle. 'So what must we do now?'

'Find the homunculus and destroy it. More important, find its operator, and see he doesn't sacrifice more girls to stay alive.'

'How?'

The Doctor went out into the hall, tore the laundry label from the basket, and carried it back into the room. 'Rundall Buildings,' he read. 'Do you know the place, Professor?'

'I'm afraid I do. It's at the centre of the most notorious part of the East End, a place of vice and squalor, long overdue for clearance.'

'It might be cleared very quickly,' said the Doctor grimly. 'Weng-Chiang, as he calls himself, is like a monkey playing with matches in a gun-powder barrel. A scientific ignoramus who doesn't appreciate the dangers of Zygma energy. If he tampers with that Time

Cabinet he'll blow up most of London.'

This was a danger that Litefoot could understand. 'Then we must stop him, Doctor.' He rose to his feet, staggered and sat down again hurriedly.

The Doctor put a hand on his shoulder. 'You're still not fit, Professor. You must stay here and rest. Leela and I will go.'

'You can't take a young woman to that place! At this hour of the night she'll witness the vilest scenes of depravity.'

'She's already encountered Weng-Chiang himself, Professor. And nothing could be viler than that.'

Mr Sin sat on his little throne, following the movements of his master with black glittering eyes. Greel stood beside the Time Cabinet, running his fingers caressingly over its surface. He looked round him in satisfaction. He was in the secret headquarters prepared for him by the Tong, a long low room, ornately furnished in the style of a Chinese temple. At the far end steps led up to a huge Dragon idol on a raised dais, its huge saucer-eyes glaring balefully over the room. Greel's scientific equipment had been re-assembled on the waiting laboratory benches, and all around, the black-clad servants of the Tong prostrated themselves before their god, the great Weng-Chiang.

'Liberation, Mr Sin,' said Greel exultantly. 'Freedom! I can become whole again. How I have dreamt of this moment. I can be free of this dying body, re-fashion myself in some distant time and place. Now that we have the Time Cabinet, we shall not stay long in this barbarous century.' He snapped his fingers: Lee, who had now replaced Chang as Greel's chief servant, hurried forward and bowed. 'The bag,' said Greel impatiently.

'What bag, Lord?'

'I brought it from the chamber beneath the cellar. I ordered you to bring it here, with the other sacred things.'

Lee bowed his head. 'Lord, there was much trouble when the body of the man Casey was found. Many people came to the cellar. I fled. The bag was left behind.'

Greel smashed him to the ground with one savage blow. 'You know the penalty for failing me. Up—and take the sting of the scorpion!'

Greel produced a jewelled box in which lay a small black pill. He stared hynotically at Lee who reached out, took the pill from the box and swallowed it. His body went rigid, he gave a single choked cry and fell dead at Greel's feet.

Greel glared malevolently at the terrified group. 'You have seen the penalty of failure,' he hissed. 'Now, return to the theatre, and *bring me that bag*!'


Jago stood in the theatre cellar looking thoughtfully around him. The evening had ended in disaster as far as the performance was concerned. With the death of poor Casey, and the disappearance of Chang, he had been forced to cancel the performance—*and* refund the audience's money. Before he could open again he had to find a top-ranking act from somewhere to put on the top of the bill. Despite all these problems, Jago was in a cheerful mood. The more he thought about it, the more convinced he became that his latest bright idea was a real winner.

'Shilling a head,' he muttered to himself. 'Guinea a head, more like it! Tours round the lair of the phantom! Personally conducted by yours truly, one of the heroes of the whole affair. The ladies will swoon in

my arms! I'll get all this junk cleared out, call in the
Electric Light Company ...' Full of plans for a prosperous future, Jago began striding about the cellar—
and fell sprawling over some bulky object. Picking
himself up, he saw that the obstacle was a bulky carpet-
bag. It was incredibly heavy, and it took all Jago's
strength to lug it clear of the pile of junk. He opened
it and found it full of strange-looking machinery. Resting on top was a saucer-shaped crystal pendant. Jago
shook his head wonderingly, and closed the bag again.
He stood thinking for a moment. The trap-door to
Greel's chamber had been left standing open, and
suddenly a dragging sound came from below. Jago
looked nervously at the trap-door, grabbed the heavy
bag and lugged it up the cellar steps. As he disappeared, the sound of hoarse, painful breathing came
from down below. A grimy yellow hand appeared over
the edge of the trap, clawing feebly for a hold ...

Professor Litefoot was doing his best to sort out the
shambles the band of Tong assassins had made of his
living-room. He could well have left the job to the servants, but Litefoot was a tidy soul, and couldn't bear
disorder. He took off his coat, rolled up his sleeves,
and strapping on one of Mrs Hudson's old aprons, he
set about the job of tidying up.

He was sweeping up the remains of a once-valuable
porcelain statuette when he heard a knocking on the
door.

He looked at the clock, and hesitated for a moment.
The police had taken away the body of their unfortunate colleague, accepting Litefoot's assurances that
there was no further need for a guard on the door. As
the knocking came again, Litefoot wondered if he had
been wise to dispense with police protection.

He went slowly into the hall, chose a heavy walking stick from the stand and cautiously opened the door. Facing him was a bulky red-faced figure in full evening dress, carrying, with some difficulty, an enormous carpet-bag.

Litefoot stared at his unexpected visitor in astonishment. 'May I ask who you are, sir?'

Jago saw a tall beaky-nosed old fellow in an apron, with a brush in one hand, and a walking stick in the other, and naturally assumed that he was addressing Litefoot's butler. He strode confidently past him, and set the bag down in the hall. 'Thank you, my man. Tell your master that Mr Jago wishes to see him urgently. Chop, chop, man, hurry up and announce me.'

'Consider yourself announced,' said the Professor acidly. 'I'm Litefoot!'

Jago reeled, but recovered immediately. 'I should have realised—that brow, those hands. England's peerless professor of pathology.' He swept off his top hat with a flourish. 'Henry Gordon Jago, sir, at your service!'

Litefoot decided his visitor was either mad or drunk. 'Just tell me what all this is about, sir,' he demanded.

'It is about the Doctor,' said Jago with impressive dignity. 'The Doctor—and this bag. Shall we go inside?'

Heaving up the bag he marched into the sitting-room, and Litefoot had no alternative but to follow. Jago sat in the best armchair, looked hopefully at the decanter, accepted a large brandy and told the Professor of his association with the Doctor. 'When I found the bag in my cellar,' he concluded, 'I was sure the Doctor would be interested. I inquired for him at the police station, and they told me he had been last seen in your company—so here I am. A great pleasure to be associated with you in this devilish affair.'

Litefoot looked dubiously at the bag. 'I'm sure the Doctor will be very interested. Unforunately he isn't here at present.'

'I know, I know,' said Jago. 'The sleuth who never rests, eh?'

Litefoot smiled. 'He did once remark that sleep was for tortoises.' He opened the bag and peered inside. 'You know, for the life of me, I can't discern what all this strange apparatus might be used for. I gather you think it belongs to this murderous lunatic the Doctor is hunting?'

'Well, it's nothing to do with my theatre, Professor, of that I'm sure.'

Litefoot tugged thoughtfully at his moustache. 'Presumably it was left behind by accident—which means that someone might well return for it.'

Jago nodded shrewdly. 'A good point, Professor. We must mention that to the Doctor.'

'We can do better than that, Mr Jago. We can take a hand ourselves. If we keep a discreet watch on your theatre, we might be able to spot these villains and trail them to their lair.'

Jago got hurriedly to his feet. 'A splendid scheme, Professor. Unfortunately the nocturnal vapours are bad for my chest and ...'

Ruthlessly Litefoot over-rode his evasions. 'Don't worry about that, man, I'll lend you a nice heavy cape. Just write a little note for the Doctor, and we can be on our way. You'll find pen and paper on the desk over there.'

Jago saw there was no escape. 'Thank you, Professor,' he said faintly and began to write.

Litefoot picked up his cudgel and waved it fiercely through the air. 'We might just be lucky tonight, Mr Jago. And if we are, I've quite a few lumps to repay!'

The Doctor gave a final heave on his burglar's jemmy, and the skylight cracked open. 'Come on, Leela,' he whispered, and dropped down inside. Leela swung her legs through the skylight and dropped down after him.

They had arrived at the laundry building to find it locked, barred and apparently deserted. The Doctor, in no mood to be delayed, had promptly climbed up on to the low roof and broken in. Now they were in a long corridor, piled high with laundry baskets. There was a door at the end, but it proved to be locked. The Doctor peered through the keyhole and saw that the key was in the lock on the other side.

He snatched some wrapping paper from one of the baskets and slid it under the door. Then he took a pencil from his pocket and poked it into the lock, pushing the key out on the other side. The key fell on to the paper, the Doctor drew paper and key back through the gap under the door, picked up the key, opened the door and ushered Leela through.

They entered a long dusty room divided into cubicles by curtains of sacking. Inside each cubicle a rough straw mattress lay on the floor. The Doctor looked round. 'Sleeping quarters for the Tong,' he whispered.

Leela sniffed. 'That smell . . . what is it?'

'Pipe of poppy—opium! A narcotic.' He looked round the deserted room. 'Apparently the Tong have another warren—which means Weng-Chiang will soon be up to his tricks again.'

'He will sacrifice more girls?'

'He'll need to build up his strength before using the Time Cabinet. He's got to kill again—tonight. But where is he?'

From somewhere nearby a weak voice whispered. 'At the House of the Dragon, Doctor.'

## 13

## The House of the Dragon

The Doctor whirled round and ripped the sacking curtain from a nearby cubicle. Stretched out on a straw mattress lay Chang, placidly smoking a long, thin wooden pipe. He was a very different figure from the elegant magician who had dominated the stage of the Palace Theatre. His robes were ragged and filthy now, his face grimy and grey with weariness, and his left leg was a bundle of blood-soaked rags.

'Good evening, Mr Chang,' said the Doctor gently. 'We thought you had already gone to join your ancestors.'

'Not yet, Doctor ... not quite. Though I shall certainly do so before very long.' Chang gestured feebly towards his leg. The Doctor moved to take off the wrappings, wondering if he could still help, but Chang waved him angrily away. 'No,·Doctor, it is too late. And thanks to the opium, I feel no pain.'

Leela shuddered, remembering her own encounter with the giant rat. It was easy to imagine what those terrible jaws had done to Chang's leg. 'How did you escape from it?' she asked.

Chang spoke in a quiet, placid voice, as if describing events that had happened to someone else, a long time ago. 'When the rat seized my leg, I fainted with fear. I was unconscious when it dragged me away. I awoke in a charnel house of bones and putrefying remains.'

The Doctor nodded. 'The thing couldn't have been

hungry. It was saving you for later—rats don't keep a very tidy larder.'

Chang went on calmly. 'I lay in that place of horror and cursed my benefactor Weng-Chiang, who had brought me to such a fate. Hatred gave me the strength to drag myself here. I planned to destroy my false god —the last act of the great Weng-Chiang. But there was no one here. The rats had fled.'

'You should have destroyed him long ago,' said Leela sternly.

'Perhaps. But I believed in him. Just as I believed in myself, the great magician Li H'sen Chang.'

'It was a good act,' said the Doctor gently. 'One of the best I've ever seen.'

Chang smiled bitterly. 'Until Weng-Chiang shamed me. The whole theatre saw my failure. I lost face...'

Chang's voice faded, and the Doctor leaned forward urgently. 'Tell me about the House of the Dragon.'

Chang's voice was very feeble. 'Soon the Great Chang was to have performed before the Queen Empress ... me, the son of a peasant ...'

'The House of the Dragon, Chang? Where is it?'

Chang struggled to focus his eyes on the Doctor. 'It is his Temple and his fortress, prepared for him by the Tong.' Chang struggled to sit up. 'Beware the Eye of the Dragon, Doctor,' he cried, and slumped back on to the mattress.

The Doctor shook him gently. 'Li H'sen! Where is it?'

Now Chang's voice was a feeble whisper. 'Soon I shall rejoin my ancestors. Already I see them, walking to greet me from the Palace of Jade ... Now I shall cross the golden bridge of the gods.'

'The address, Chang,' shouted the Doctor.

Chang made a last effort to speak, but no words

came out. He pitched forward on the mattress, and lay quite still.

'He is dead,' said Leela flatly.

The Doctor sighed. 'And he's left us with a Chinese puzzle. Well there's no point in staying here. Let's get back to the Professor.'


Mr Sin sat, smiling as ever, on his throne beside the dragon stool. Beside him stood Greel, waiting impatiently. Black-clad members of the Tong entered the room and prostrated themselves before him. 'Well?' he snarled. 'Where is it?'

The Tong member who had succeeded Lee as leader of the group was called Ho. He stepped forward, quaking with terror.

'Bag is gone, Lord. We look all places in theatre. Bag not there.'

Greel stormed down the steps of the throne and the terrified men scattered before him. 'You incompetent lice,' he raged. 'You crawling mindless dogs! That bag contains parts for the machine by which I live—*and the key to the Time Cabinet.* I'll find it if I have to take this accused city apart stone by stone ...' Greel's pacing about had brought him close to the window. He broke off suddenly, and stared out. When he spoke next, it was in a voice of sinister calm. 'Ho! Were you followed here?'

'Followed, Lord?'

Greel pointed to the window. Nervously Ho came nearer and looked out. Two figures lurked by the gas lamp on the corner, obviously keeping watch on the house. Greel stared hard at the two men. 'One of them is Jago, the man who owns the theatre. They must have followed you here after the search.' Greel was thinking aloud. 'They *expected* you to return to the theatre, and were waiting—*which means they have found the bag!* Bring them to me—alive!'

Jago and Litefoot stood huddled against a wall, looking up at the big detached house on the other side of the road. 'This must be their hideaway right enough,' said Litefoot. 'Damned impudence! This is a thoroughly respectable area.' It was a road of solidly built suburban residences, each set well back from the road in its own grounds—houses that were much like Litefoot's own.

The Professor's plan had worked better than he'd dared hope. They had arrived at the theatre in time to find a band of Tong assassins busily ransacking the place. Restraining the indignant Jago from calling the police, Litefoot had persuaded him to wait outside the theatre until the search was abandoned, and the villains drove away in a waiting carriage. Summoning a passing cab, Litefoot and Jago had followed their quarry across London to this quiet secluded road.

Jago rubbed his hands together to warm them. 'Pity there are too many of 'em to tackle, eh, Professor. I was just itching for a fight!'

Litefoot smiled at his companion's enthusiasm. 'Thing is, Mr Jago, what do we do now?'

'Adjourn for a little liquid refreshment?' suggested Jago hopefully. 'I know a little tavern not far from here.'

Litefoot shook his head. 'I'm afraid not. I think one of us should stay here on watch, while the other returns for the Doctor and the police.'

'Splendid idea,' said Jago promptly. 'I'll be as quick as I can, Professor.'

Litefoot touched his arm and pointed. 'Too late, I'm afraid, Mr Jago.' A ring of black-clad Chinese had appeared out of the darkness, encircling them, creeping steadily closer. 'Oh corks,' said Jago faintly.

Litefoot took a firm grip on his cudgel. 'Backs to the wall, I'm afraid, Mr Jago.'

Jago doubled his fists. 'Keep off you lot, I warn you,' he quavered. 'I'm a tiger when my dander's up!'

The Chinese came forward in a silent rush.

Litefoot and Jago fought valiantly, but they were hopelessly outnumbered. They disappeared beneath a pile of their attackers, and minutes later they were being dragged semi-conscious into the house. The heavy door slammed behind them, and the quiet suburban street was peaceful once more.

Battered and bleeding, Litefoot and Jago were thrown at Greel's feet. Jago shuddered, as the sinister figure limped towards them. At a nod from Greel, they were dragged to their feet. He glared malevolently at them. 'So, you choose to spy on the House of the Dragon? That is unwise. You will suffer for it.'

'You'll be the one to suffer once the police arrive,' said Litefoot bravely.

Greel laughed. 'The police. Do you hear that, Mr Sin? They take us for simpletons.'

Mr Sin seemed to smile on his little throne.

Jago tried to back up Litefoot's bluff. 'The police will be here, don't you worry. They're not far behind us.'

'You told them you were coming here?'

'Of course,' said Litefoot. 'We're not fools, you know.'

Greel struck him savagely across the face. 'Lies! You did not *know* where you were going. You followed my men here.' Greel sprang on Jago, and seized him by the throat. 'Why were you waiting at the theatre?'

Jago glanced desperately at his companion. 'Why were we waiting at the theatre, Litefoot?' he croaked.

Litefoot folded his arms. 'I refuse to answer. Do as you please with us.'

'I say, steady on,' gasped Jago. All very well for Litefoot to be so defiant. It wasn't his throat.

Greel tightened his grip. 'Then I will tell you. You were waiting for my men to collect the bag.'

Powerless in Greel's grip, Jago gasped. 'You're choking me . . . to death . . .'

'Exactly. Now—where is the bag?'

Jago gave a strangled cry and Litefoot shouted, 'Let him go!'

Greel squeezed harder, and Jago began sagging at the knees. 'The bag is at my house,' shouted Litefoot. 'Now for pity's sake release him.'

Greel let go of Jago, who dropped choking to the floor. 'Very well. You will both die later—and slowly. It will give pleasure to my servants.' Greel gestured to the watching members of the Tong. 'Now put them with the other prisoners—and prepare my carriage! We have work to do.'

The Doctor was reading Jago's note out loud to Leela.

'My dear Doctor,

Contained in this capacious carpet-bag which I discovered inadvertently in the cellar is a collection of sundry items of a baffling nature.

The Professor and I are keeping observation on the theatre, and shortly hope to report to you the whereabouts of the mysterious Weng-Chiang.

Your fellow detective,
H.G.J.'

'What does it mean, Doctor?'

'It means they're in trouble,' said the Doctor rue-fully. He opened the bag and rummaged inside. 'Spare parts for an organic distillation set-up by the look of it—aha!'

The Doctor took a saucer-shaped pendant from the bag and held it up exultantly. 'Eureka! Do you know what this is, Leela?'

Leela gave him a look. 'You ask only so that you can tell me.'

'It's the trionic lattice for the Time Cabinet. It's impossible to open it without it.'

'You mean it is a key?'

'Exactly. Our black-masked friend isn't just a scientific fool, he's absent-minded too. First he has the key without the Cabinet. Now he's got the Cabinet without the key!'

'Perhaps he has another Eureka?'

The Doctor grinned. 'Eureka is Greek for "This bath is too hot",' he said obscurely. 'No, there can't be another key of this combination.'

'In that case, he will return to the theatre. We must go.'

The Doctor didn't move, and Leela looked reprovingly at him. 'Our friends are in danger, Doctor. We must help them.'

The Doctor pointed to the ashes in the grate. The coal had burned away to a fine ash. 'Litefoot keeps a good fire—so we know he's been out of the house for some time. We'll do no good rushing all over London looking for Weng-Chiang. Much easier to wait for him to come here.'

Leela stood very still, frowning in concentration. 'When our enemy finds the bag has been taken from the theatre ... he will soon discover that Litefoot and Jago are watching him. He will capture them, force

114

them to tell him where it is—and return here to find it!'

'You're learning to think at last.'

'You thought of all that at once, Doctor?'

'Well, almost at once,' said the Doctor modestly.

Leela looked relieved. 'For a moment I thought you feared to attack our enemy. Where shall we set our ambush?' She went over to the side cabinet and took one of Litefoot's carving knives from a drawer. She found a sharpening stone, and began putting a better edge on the knife. Happily she looked up at the Doctor. 'It is time that we did battle with this underground crab!'

Litefoot and Jago had been thrown into a gas-lit basement kitchen and locked in. Two young women lay unconscious against the wall, and Litefoot was examining them.

Jago looked on gloomily. 'Are they dead, Professor?'

'Drugged, I'd say. He must send those fiends of his to kidnap them off the streets. What unspeakable horror must lie behind that mask he wears.' Litefoot sighed despondently, and began pacing about the room. 'Afraid I don't see any way out of this, Jago. I think we're done for.'

Jago tried to be optimistic. 'You're forgetting the Doctor, Professor. He's a trained investigator, remember. A speck of mud, a fleck of paint ... clues like that speak volumes to a great detective. I'll wager he's on our track this very minute.'

Litefoot stopped his pacing. 'I say, Jago, look at this.' He pointed to a panel in the wall. 'One of those service hatches. Dumb waiters they call 'em.'

'Professor, I don't see how you can think of food at a time like this——'

'My dear man, I'm not thinking of food. We can take the shelves out, squeeze inside and make our escape from this room.'

'By Jiminy, you're right,' said Jago exultantly. 'We'll outwit the blighters yet.'

Hurriedly they pulled out the shelves and with some difficulty squeezed themselves inside the service hatch.

'Those ropes don't look too sound,' said Jago apprehensively.

Litefoot smiled. 'He that is down need fear no fall, Mr Jago. A quotation from Bunyan.'

'Very consoling,' said Jago gloomily.

Litefoot seized a rope and Jago did the same. 'Right, *heave*! And *heave*...'

With much puffing and groaning they hauled the hatch up the chute, until at last they were opposite the hatch on the floor above. They shoved it open and sprang out—to find themselves in what appeared to be a Chinese temple. From the top of a flight of steps a dragon idol leered malevolently down at them.

'This isn't the dining-room,' whispered Jago.

'It isn't the way out either,' said Litefoot sadly. He pointed towards the door. Two enormous Tong hatchet men were advancing menacingly towards them.

Jago sighed. 'Well never mind, Professor. At least we tried.'


Leela studied the layout of the dining-room, considering how to set her ambush. 'We should try to trap them in a crossfire, Doctor...'

To Leela's annoyance the Doctor didn't seem to be taking her combat preparations very seriously. He pointed to a bowl of nuts on a side table. 'A crossfire of what? Hazelnuts? Bread pellets?'

'Surely the Professor must have weapons here? In

a place this size, there must be fixed strongpoints to defend the approaches...'

The Doctor grinned affectionately at her. 'I've brought you to the wrong century. You'd have loved Agincourt. Stay here, I'll see what I can find.'

The Doctor left the room and began rummaging under the stairs, wondering where Litefoot kept the fowling piece that had done so well against the giant rat.

Alone in the dining-room, Leela stood with her back to the curtains, gazing thoughtfully around the room. She didn't see the long-nailed claw-like hand that appeared around the edge of the curtain. It was holding a pad of soft material.

Suddenly Greel sprang out from behind the curtain and clapped the pad over Leela's face. She struggled wildly, but within seconds her head was swimming from the effects of the chloroform. With the last of her strength she wriggled round and clawed desperately at Greel, ripping the black-leather mask from his face.

At the sight of what lay beneath the mask, Leela froze in horror. Greel's face was warped, distorted, *bent*, eyes, nose and mouth jumbled nightmarishly together, like a plasticine face squashed by a fist. Leela had only a moment to take in the terrible sight. The pad came down over her face, and she sank into unconsciousness.

# 14

# The Prisoners of Greel

When the Doctor came back into the room some few minutes later, there was no sign of Leela. Greel, his mask now back in place, stood waiting by the curtained window.

The Doctor beamed, apparently unsurprised. 'Ah, good! We've been waiting for you.'

'On the contrary, Doctor, it is we who are waiting for you.' Greel gestured towards the door and the Doctor turned. Mr Sin stalked into the room. Behind him came a little group of Tong hatchet men, one of them supporting the unconscious Leela.

'Life's little surprises,' said the Doctor softly. His voice hardened as he looked at Leela. 'What have you done to her?'

'Nothing—yet.'

'Take my advice—don't,' said the Doctor quietly.

'*Your* advice?' Greel gave a scornful laugh. 'You are an unusual man, Doctor, but in opposing me you have gone far out of your depth. You have something of mine, I believe. I want it back.'

'Something of yours? Now what could it be, I wonder? I borrow so many things and forget where I put them. Terrible habit.'

Greel tapped the carpet bag. 'The Time Key was in this bag. It is not there now. Give it to me.'

The Doctor began a pantomime of patting all his pockets, muttering. 'Time Key, Time Key, now where did I put the wretched thing—ah!'

Greel leaned forward eagerly. The Doctor produced a paper bag and held it out. 'Forgotten I had these. Care for a jelly baby?'

Greel struck his hand aside. 'I will give you three seconds, Doctor, then Mr Sin will kill the girl.'

Knife raised, Mr Sin began stalking towards Leela with jerky eagerness. Greel began counting. 'One ... Two ... Three. Kill her.'

Mr Sin raised his knife—and the Doctor produced the saucer-shaped pendant from his pocket. 'This what you want—the trionic lattice?'

Greel stretched out a claw-like hand. 'Give it to me!'

The Doctor drew back the pendant, holding it just out of reach. 'Careful—you nearly made me drop it.' He studied the pendant thoughtfully. 'Very fragile, this crystalline structure. Probably shatter into a thousand pieces, if I dropped it and trod on it ...' He tossed the pendant carelessly from one hand to the other.

'You arrogant jackanapes,' snarled Greel. 'I will have you killed ...'

The hatchet men surged forward eagerly, and the Doctor held the pendant high. 'Call off your dogs. I get nervous when I'm crowded.'

Greel waved the Chinese back, and the Doctor smiled. 'That's better.'

Greel pointed a skinny finger at Leela. 'Give me the Time Key and I will spare her life.'

The Doctor swung the pendant. 'I never trusted men with long, dirty fingernails.'

Greel was nearing the end of his patience. 'You can trust me to kill you if you do not obey me. Give me the Time Key.'

The Doctor swung the pendant to and fro. 'I'll make a bargain with you. You can have your Time Key back when we reach the House of the Dragon.'

'What trickery is this?'

'I think you're holding two friends of mine prisoner?'

'The two blundering dolts who spied on me? Yes, I have them.'

The Doctor nodded, pleased to learn that Litefoot and Jago were still alive.

'I want them released as well. When we're *all* free, I'll hand over the Time Key—and not before.'

Greel nodded slowly. 'Very well.'

'Right, then. You and your chaps can lead the way.'

Greel picked up Mr Sin, and turned to the Tong hatchet men. 'Bring the bag—and the girl.'

The Doctor said firmly, 'The bag by all means. The girl stays here.'

'You would be wise not to press me too far, Doctor.'

The Doctor held up the pendant. 'Just lead the way.'

Greel nodded to the Chinese holding Leela. They let her go, and she slumped to the floor. Greel swept out, followed by his hatchet men. The Doctor paused, and looked down at Leela. Her eyes opened and she looked steadily at him for a moment, and then closed them again. The Doctor smiled, and followed the others from the house.

As soon as the front door closed behind them, Leela climbed quickly to her feet and moved quietly out of the room.


Escape attempt thwarted, Jago and Litefoot had been thrown back into their kitchen prison for what seemed hours of waiting.

Litefoot heard a bustle of movement and went to listen at the door. 'Seems to be something happening. Sounds as if a big group of people are coming into the house.'

'More Wongs for the Tong,' said Jago gloomily.

Litefoot looked at his watch. 'It'll soon be dawn.'

Jago looked alarmed. 'I say, that's when these chaps —do things, isn't it? Sacrifice their victims?'

'You're thinking of Druids, old chap.'

Jago seemed unconvinced. 'I've been worrying, rather. Can't seem to stop myself. You see, the trouble with me, Litefoot ... I know I talk a lot. But I'm not so jolly brave when it comes to it, old man. Try to be ... but I'm not.'

Litefoot nodded understandingly. 'When it comes to it, I don't suppose anyone is.'

'Thought I'd better tell you ... in case I let the side down.'

Litefoot clapped him on the shoulder. 'You won't, Henry. I know you won't.'


The Doctor looked admiringly round the Dragon Room, as Greel set Mr Sin on his throne by the Dragon idol. He stared hard into the manikin's unwinking eyes as if transmitting some silent signal, and Mr Sin's head gave the faintest of nods. Satisfied, Greel turned to Ho. 'Bring the prisoners here.'

The Doctor had wandered over to Greel's re-assembled organic distillation set-up, and was studying it thoughtfully. As Greel moved towards him he turned and said cheerfully, 'Very impressive. I'll take the birds'-nest soup. This *is* where you do the cooking isn't it?'

Greel moved so that his body blocked the Doctor's view of Mr Sin. Behind him the manikin was crawling into a concealed hatchway set into the idol's side.

'You cannot hope to understand its function, Doctor. It is part of a technology far beyond your time.'

'Just simple old-fashioned cannibalism,' said the

Doctor scornfully. 'This machine just saves you from having to chew the gristly bits.'

'It contains the secret of life——'

'Rubbish,' interrupted the Doctor. 'Degenerate bunkum! Your superior technology is no more than the twisted lunacy of a scientific Dark Age.' Suddenly the Doctor swung round. 'Where's your pig-brained Peking Homunculus got to?'

'I have no further need of Mr Sin,' said Greel smoothly. 'I have dismissed him.' To distract the Doctor's attention, Greel moved to a side table on which stood a chessboard set out with ornately carved Chinese chessmen. He made an opening move. Almost automatically, the Doctor moved to the other side of the board and countered it.

Greel moved another piece. 'You know the secret of Mr Sin's construction, Doctor? How can you, in the nineteenth century, know the secrets of the fifty-first?'

Almost without looking at the board, the Doctor moved another piece, 'I was with the Philippino army during the final battle for Reykjavik.'

'You lie!' hissed Greel, as he moved again.

The Doctor studied the board. 'Now listen, what's-your-name—what *did* you call yourself before you started posing as a Chinese god?'

'I am Magnus Greel,' said the black-cloaked figure proudly.

The Doctor stretched his hand towards the board. 'So, you're Greel ... the infamous Minister of Justice of the Supreme Alliance. The butcher of Brisbane...'

It was all becoming clear now, thought the Doctor. Greel had created the murderous homunculus with the deliberate intention of triggering off a World War. When the conflict had erupted, Greel and his allies were ready. For a time the Supreme Alliance, a league of ruthless dictators, had ruled most of the Earth. Finally an alliance of their victims had risen against them, crushing them at the terrible battle of Reykjavik...

After the battle Greel had disappeared, taking the homunculus with him. He had been hunted as a War Criminal, but had never been found. Now the mystery of his disappearance had been solved. Fleeing in his newly-developed Time Cabinet he had landed, more or less at random, in nineteenth-century China. Weak and sick from the terrible distorting effects of the Zygma beam, he had sheltered in Li H'sen Chang's hut. Meanwhile the Time Cabinet had been taken by the Emperor's soldiers, given as a present to Litefoot's family, and finished up in Victorian England.

Ever since then Greel must have been striving to recover the Cabinet, handicapped by the recurrent wasting sickness caused by the effects of the Zygma beam. A sickness which could only be held off by the constant supply of young human victims, forced to sacrifice their life essence to keep Magnus Greel alive. Now it appeared that Greel was on the verge of yet another escape, with all his terrible crimes still unpunished...

All these reflections from a history that had yet to happen flashed through the Doctor's mind while he was reaching for his Queen. He moved it forward and said quietly, 'Checkmate, I think.'

Greel's arm flashed out, sweeping the pieces from the board. 'It is *impossible* for you to know these things, Doctor.'

The Doctor looked at him with distaste. 'Is it, Greel? I know you're a war criminal from the future, that a hundred thousand deaths can be laid at your door.'

'Enemies of the state. They were used in the advancement of science.'

'They were slaughtered in filthy machines like that —part of your quest for eternal life!'

Greel felt compelled to defend himself. 'If you are from the future, you are here because of my work. So, I am remembered only as a war criminal? The winning side writes the history, Doctor. *You* could not be here if it were not for my work.' He waved towards the Time Cabinet. 'I made this possible, I found the resources, the scientists...'

'That abortion?' said the Doctor scornfully. 'Your Zygma beam experiments were a hopeless failure, Greel.'

'I used the cabinet to travel through Time,' screamed Greel. 'I escaped from my enemies.'

'And look what it did to you!'

'There was a temporal distortion of the metabolism. It can be adjusted...' Greel broke off, as Litefoot and Jago were thrust into the room. At the sight of the Doctor, Jago brightened immediately.

'By Jingo, Litefoot, didn't I tell you?' He turned sternly towards Greel. 'The game's up, my friend. We have the place surrounded.'

'I'm afraid we don't, Mr Jago,' said the Doctor. 'All we have at the moment is a rather precarious understanding.'

'I have kept my word, Doctor,' said Greel impatiently. 'Your friends are here. Now give me the Time Key.'

'Not until they're safe out of the house.' The Doctor turned to Jago and Litefoot. 'Off you go—and hurry.'

Jago was already heading for the door, but Litefoot hesitated. 'Doctor, there are two wretched girls downstairs...'

'Take them with you then. Now go!'

Litefoot hurried after Jago, and Greel glared balefully at the Doctor. 'Your demands become too great, Doctor.' Suddenly Greel stepped to one side, leaving the Doctor standing directly in line with the Dragon idol. There was a sudden crackle of power, and a ray of green light stabbed from the Dragon's eyes. Caught by its blast, the Doctor staggered and fell—and Greel snatched the pendant from his hand as he crumpled to the floor.

# 15

# The Firebomb

The Dragon's head swung down, as if to blast the Doctor again, but Greel held up his hand. 'Enough. I want him alive.'

Inside the Dragon, Mr Sin reluctantly removed his hands from the laser-controls, angry because he had not been allowed to kill.

Litefoot had run back into the room, and was kneeling beside the Doctor, whose face was drawn from the effects of the tremendous shock. 'Doctor,' he asked anxiously. 'Are you all right?'

The Doctor opened his eyes with a tremendous effort. 'Beware the Eye of the Dragon,' he whispered and fell back unconscious.

Greel waved to the awe-stricken Tong guards who stood waiting by the door. 'Take them!'

Two guards began dragging the Doctor's body away, while others hustled Litefoot and Jago out of the room. Greel was left alone and triumphant, the Time Key in his hand.

In a corridor at the rear of the building, a Tong guard padded silently towards the back of the house. He had heard faint, suspicious sounds, and was going to investigate.

As he passed a curtained alcove Leela stepped out, took his neck in a choking grip, and dragged him into the alcove. The curtains billowed frantically for a moment, and were still.

Mr Sin sat patiently inside the head of the Dragon. Through the sights of the laser-ray, he could see Greel moving towards the Time Cabinet. Swivelling the sighting-mechanism to keep his master in view, Mr Sin reached out and stroked the firing-controls...

With loving care, Greel pressed the Time Key into the recess in the front of the Cabinet. There was a hum of power and the door slid open. Most of the inside of the Cabinet was taken up with complicated yet curiously ramshackle equipment. Greel, however, seemed well-satisfied as he checked over the controls. 'Everything exactly as it was ... The Parallax synchrons fully charged, the chronos tubes set at maximum...'

With absorbed intensity, Greel began preparing for his departure. 'The Doctor was wrong,' he muttered. 'My Zygma experiment was a success. A complete success! Soon I shall be free once more.'


Thrown back into captivity, Litefoot went on trying to revive the unconscious Doctor. Jago looked on, and the two girls stared dully ahead of them. It was perhaps as well they had no idea of where they were or what was happening to them.

'How is he?' asked Jago worriedly.

Litefoot looked up. 'There's a curious double heartbeat ... but there doesn't seem to be any real damage.'

'Struck down from behind by a dastardly device,' said Jago fiercely.

'Sssh! I think he's trying to say something...'

Suddenly, the Doctor spoke. 'There's a one-eyed yellow idol to the North of Katmandu. There's a little marble cross below the town...'

'By jove, he's reciting Kipling,' whispered Jago.

The Doctor opened his eyes. 'Nonsense, it's Harry

Champion. Kipling used to get very annoyed about that.' He struggled to his feet. 'How long was I unconscious?'

'Just a few minutes,' said Litefoot. 'A remarkable recovery, Doctor.'

The Doctor stretched and took a few paces around the room. Jago looked on admiringly. 'What an iron constitution!'

The Doctor went over to the bed and examined the two dull-eyed girls. 'The broth of oblivion,' he muttered. Straightening up, he stood looking round the room deep in thought.

'Surely there's something we can do, Doctor?' asked Litefoot.

The Doctor smiled. 'There's always something, Professor. For a start, put those two unfortunate ladies in the corner over there.' Jago and Litefoot moved the unresisting girls, and the Doctor examined the mattress on which they had been sitting. 'Excellent, good thick linen. It'll do very well.' He saw Jago and Litefoot looking at him expectantly. 'Don't waste time, gentlemen. Help me to wrench that gas pipe away from the wall.'


Greel made a final adjustment, and stepped back from the Time Cabinet. 'All is ready. Time to prepare my two partridges.' With gruesome good humour, Greel called over to the Dragon idol. 'Why don't you come out of there, Mr Sin? Sulking because I wouldn't let you kill the Doctor? You shall kill him soon enough— when I have drained every atom of his knowledge of the Zygma process. Kill them all if you wish, before we leave. As soon as I have re-established my metabolic balance, I shall enter the Zygma beam for the second time. This time there will be no mistake...'

Engrossed in his plans for escape, Greel failed to see Leela as, knife in hand, she slipped silently into the room and hid behind a laboratory bench.

Suddenly Greel moved away from the Cabinet and went to a gong that hung close to the door. Leela realised her danger too late. Greel was about to summon more of his Tong hatchet men. Well, at least she could kill him before they had time to arrive.

As Greel struck the gong, Leela jumped upon the bench and launched herself across the room in a flying leap. The gong-note was still hanging in the air as she landed on Greel's shoulders, bearing him to the ground. They fought wildly for a moment, but Leela was full of savage anger. Pinning Greel to the ground she brought her knife blade to his throat. 'Die, bentface!' she hissed.

Greel tried to hold back her arm, but the knife blade came ever-closer. 'No,' pleaded Greel. 'Spare me ...'

As Leela tensed her muscles for the final thrust, the room was suddenly full of black-clad Tong hatchet men. They pulled her from their Master, wrenching the knife from her hand, and held her helplessly captive. Greel staggered to his feet and hobbled towards her, snatching Leela's knife from the hatchet man who had taken it. 'Hold her still,' he commanded. His voice was hoarse with rage, and the memory of his own fear. 'Twice this she-devil has tried to kill me. *Twice!*'

With deliberate slowness, Greel brought the blade to Leela's throat. Then he threw it to the ground. 'No! I have a more fitting fate for you. *You* shall be the first morsel to feed my regeneration. Put her in the distillation chamber!'

Tong guards dragged the struggling Leela across to the machine. 'Kill me how you please,' she shouted. 'I do not fear death—unlike you, bent-face!'

Greel flinched at the memory of how he had begged

for mercy. He watched with malevolent satisfaction as the guard thrust Leela into the chamber, securing the doors so that only her head was visible, framed between the two metal spheres.

Greel went over to the machine, and stared into Leela's eyes. 'Well, tigress, now it is your turn to beg.'

'*I* shall not plead,' said Leela scornfully. 'But I swear this to you. When we are both in the great Hereafter, I shall hunt you down and force you through my agony a thousand times.'

Recoiling from the force of her anger, Greel shouted, 'Silence her.'

One of the Chinese thrust a gag into Leela's mouth. 'Bring the other girls here,' ordered Greel, and the guards hurried from the room.


Jago and Litefoot had been working hard under the Doctor's direction. Now they stood back and looked at the results. The Doctor's scheme was simple—and appallingly dangerous. The mattress-cover, now serving as a kind of cloth balloon, was hanging by the door, gas hissing into it from the broken pipe to which it was tied. From the bottom of the mattress dangled a long strip of cloth, the fuse for the Doctor's homemade firebomb.

The bed on which the mattress had once rested was tipped on its side across one corner, the water-soaked mattress propped against it for added protection. Behind the improvised shield the two girls were crouching. By now they were sufficiently revived to understand their danger, and obey the Doctor's instructions.

Jago watched the billowing of the mattress-cover as the gas hissed into it. 'It's leaking,' he said worriedly. 'I can smell it.'

'Bound to be some leakage,' said the Doctor cheerily. 'Not enough to worry about.' He wasn't nearly so optimistic as he tried to sound. Setting off a gas explosion in such a confined space would be almost as dangerous for the prisoners as for their enemies. But a single devastating stroke was needed, to dispose of as many guards as possible before they tackled Greel himself.

'It isn't that I'm *worried*,' said Jago hurriedly, 'but I'd hate to be gassed before we get a chance to see if this stunt works!'

The Doctor gave him a reassuring smile. 'Greel won't keep us waiting long. He needs his nourishment.'

'His what?'

'Greel is dying. His body is constantly wasting away. He is trying to cheat death by feeding upon the life-force of others.' He glanced at the two women in the corner, and then at Litefoot. 'You understand me, Professor?'

'I think so—the principle, at least.'

'The principle is false, in any case. All Greel achieves is a postponement of the inevitable.'

Jago interrupted them. 'Listen, Doctor. I think they're coming.'

'Then you know what to do. Your matches please, Professor.'

Litefoot and Jago joined the two men behind the bed. The Doctor called softly to the two girls. 'Now remember, you two, get out of this house just as soon as you can, and don't stop running till you're a mile away.' Too terrified to speak, both girls nodded.

The footsteps were at the door now. The Doctor lit a match, touched it to the fuse and joined the huddled group in the corner. 'Up troops and at 'em, eh?' whispered Jago excitedly.

They watched the flickering yellow flame run up

131

the strip of linen. Just as the door was flung open, it touched the gas-filled mattress cover.

There was an astonishingly loud explosion and the doorway disappeared in a sheet of flame. Black smoke filled the room, and when it cleared, the guards who had been nearest the door lay stunned on the floor, while the rest ran screaming down the corridor. 'Quick!' shouted the Doctor, and choking in the clouds of smoke the captives dashed into the corridor. The Doctor snatched up a hatchet from a fallen guard as he ran out of the room. Obedient to the Doctor's instructions, the two girls were already running for the back door. The Doctor led Jago and Litefoot towards the main stairs.

Busy at the controls of his organic distillation machine, Greel heard the boom of the explosion, and the screams of his guards. He hesitated, moved towards the door, then returned to the controls looking threateningly at Leela. 'Whatever has happened, there will be no escape for *you*. The talons of Greel will shred your flesh.' He stretched out his skinny hands to the main control—as the door was flung open, and the Doctor ran into the room. 'Greel,' shouted the Doctor, and threw the hatchet with all his force.

Determined on his revenge, Greel snatched at the master-lever. But the Doctor's hatchet was aimed not at Greel himself but at the main power cable of his machine. The hatchet severed the cable in a shower of sparks, and the machine went dead, just as the lever was pulled.

The Doctor ran to the cabinet and threw open the doors. Leela fell into his arms, and he snatched the gag from her mouth.

Greel was scuttling towards the Dragon idol. 'Kill,

Sin,' he screamed. 'Kill them all!'

'Down!' shouted the Doctor. He pulled Leela behind the laboratory bench just as the green ray blazed from the Dragon's eyes. There was a fierce crackle of energy, and smoke filled the air as chunks of blazing masonry were blasted from the wall.

Inside the Dragon Mr Sin was hunched over the controls, peering through the sights for a living target. Greel himself was hiding behind the dais on which the idol stood. The Doctor, Leela, Litefoot and Jago were all sheltering behind the heavy laboratory bench which stood by the door. Like two armies on the battlefield, the opposing forces had occupied opposite ends of the long room.

Greel shouted from his hiding place. 'I will spare your lives, all of you, if you will leave now.'

'Very magnanimous, Magnus,' called the Doctor.

'Then go!'

'With your trigger-happy little friend still covering us? No thank you!'

'I'm offering you your freedom, you fools!' screamed Greel.

The Doctor looked at the others. 'We'd be cut down before we reached the door.'

Leela nodded. 'I think so too. There is no truth in him.'

'We're staying put, Magnus,' shouted the Doctor.

'Then you will die here—all of you!'

The Doctor peered over the bench at the huddled figure on the steps. 'You might die first, Greel. You don't sound too healthy—and your food supply is halfway across London by now.'

Hobbling up the steps of the Dragon idol Greel snarled, 'Sin! Burn away that bench!'

The Dragon's eye glowed fiercely and the Doctor and the others ducked down as laser-bolt after laser-bolt sizzled into the bench. With every shot, a chunk of blazing wood was blasted away.

'If only I had a gun,' whispered Litefoot fiercely.

Jago nodded. 'Or even a catapult. I was a dab hand with a catapult as a nipper.'

Another chunk of wood was blasted from the bench, which by now was getting noticeably smaller. 'He is cutting down our cover, Doctor,' said Leela calmly. 'Soon one of us will be hit.'

A spasm of pain wracked Greel's deformed body. 'Hurry, Sin, hurry,' he croaked. 'There is little time left to me.'

Not all the servants of Weng-Chiang had fled after the explosion. A few of the more fanatical had stayed behind, huddling together in the basement. The sound of the laser-battle in the Dragon Room had encouraged them to emerge. The great Weng-Chiang was destroying his enemies with his magic ray. Would he not take a terrible vengeance if his servants deserted him? Gathering all the weapons they could find, the remnant of the Tong hatchet men crept towards the Dragon Room, determined to prove their loyalty while there was still time.

Dodging yet another laser-bolt, the Doctor sensed movement behind him and turned. Tong warriors, armed with hatchets, knives and revolvers were flooding into the room. Now the Doctor and his friends were caught in a crossfire between Tong and Dragon. The position was hopeless.

Inside the Dragon idol the eyes of Mr Sin blazed with excitement and pleasure. He was weary of shooting at a block of wood. Here were living targets. Gleefully he crouched over the controls and swung the sights.

The laser crackled again, and most of the tightly packed knot of Tong warriors in the doorway died with its first blast. Mr Sin fired again and again, picking off the survivors.

'Stop,' roared Greel. 'Stop, Sin, I command you. I am your master—obey me.'

Sin was deaf to all commands. Crazed with blood-lust, he mowed down the fleeing hatchet men, until the doorway was choked with their bodies.

The last of the guards twisted in the laser blast and dropped to the ground, a heavy revolver falling from his hand. It fell not too far from the bench. Leela nudged Jago and pointed.

Jago looked at the distance he would have to cover and shook his head firmly. 'Not a chance, my dear.'

'He cannot shoot at two targets at once.'

Jago's eyes widened. 'You mean if one of us draws the blighter's fire, the other can get to the gun?'

'Me,' said Leela flatly. 'Because I am quicker.'

With the Tong members all disposed of, Sin returned his attention to the bench. A well-aimed laser-bolt sheared off one leg and the bench lurched dangerously. Litefoot grabbed it. 'Can't hold it for long,' he yelled. 'Another few minutes and we're done for.'

The Doctor snatched up a hatchet. 'Ready then? All together . . . now!'

Three things happened more or less at once. Jago popped up like a jack-in-the-box, deliberately drawing Sin's fire. The Doctor hurled the hatchet at the Dragon's head. And Leela sprinted to the cover of an iron chest on the other side of the room, scooping up the revolver on the way.

Although it bounced harmlessly off the Dragon's head, the Doctor's hatchet probably saved Jago's life. The sight of it whirling towards him in the sights spoiled Sin's aim, and his laser-bolt crackled over Jago's head, as he dropped flat behind the wobbling barrier of the bench. 'I say, I say,' he gasped, in the comedian's traditional opening phrase. 'A funny thing nearly happened to me just now. Has she got the gun?'

A bullet whistled over Jago's head, and they all ducked down.

'Hey, who are you shooting at, young lady?' called Litefoot indignantly.

They heard Leela's voice from the other side of the room. 'Sorry! I've never fired one of these before!'

Leela's favourite weapon was the Sevateem crossbow with which she had grown up, though she had used a hand-blaster in an earlier adventure with the Doctor. But she had a natural affinity with weapons, and she soon worked out how to use the big revolver.

Taking careful aim she fired at the glowing eyes in the Dragon idol's head. She missed by inches, the great head swung round, and as the eyes shot out their deadly ray, and the great iron chest glowed red beneath the impact of a laser-bolt, Leela ducked down and waited her chance for another shot.

Jago helped Litefoot to support the weight of the tottering bench. Peering round the edge, the Doctor saw Greel crawling across the room towards the open Time Cabinet. He had suddenly become much feebler, and could only move with agonising slowness.

'It's no good, Greel,' shouted the Doctor. 'You're finished.'

Painfully Greel lifted his head. 'I can still escape you, Doctor, as I escaped my enemies before.' He inched nearer the Time Cabinet.

'Don't try it, Greel.' warned the Doctor. 'If you activate the Zygma beam it will mean certain death for all of us.'

'Lies, Doctor! Lies!' shrieked Greel.

'Listen to me. The Zygma beam is at full stretch. Try to trigger it again and it will collapse. There'll be a huge implosion, and you'll be at the centre of it. The

Zygma experiment was a disastrous failure!'

Greel's enormous vanity would not allow him to accept the truth. 'It was a success, Doctor. A total, brilliant success.'

Greel was at the Time Cabinet now, and about to step inside. He saw the Dragon's head swing towards *him*.

'Sin, no!' he screamed. But Sin's blood-lust was totally in control now. To him Greel was just another living target. Greel dropped behind the cabinet as a laser-bolt sizzled past him.

Sin's attempt to kill Greel gave Leela her chance. Leaping to her feet she held the revolver in both hands, took careful aim and squeezed the trigger. The heavy bullet blasted through the focussing crystal that was the Dragon's eye, and the head of the idol exploded in smoke and flame.

Greel leaped to his feet and sprang for the cabinet, but the Doctor was too quick for him. He grappled with Greel, pulling him back from the Time Cabinet. They struggled for a moment, then Greel called up the last of his failing strength. With a frantic lunge he broke free of the Doctor's grip, staggered forward and crashed into the jumble of electronic machinery that filled the centre of the cabinet. There was a blaze of fierce blue sparks, a muffled explosion. Blasted from the cabinet, Greel crashed to the ground.

They all gathered round the huddled black-clad figure. Through the slits of the mask Greel's eyes stared sightlessly up at them.

'Is bent-face dead?' asked Leela.

Litefoot glanced curiously at her. 'Why do you call him bent-face?'

'Because he is!'

Curiously Litefoot reached out for the mask, but

the Doctor gently restrained him. 'I shouldn't, Professor.'

'Why not?'

'Look!'

Greel's prostrate body was collapsing, crumbling, dwindling away to dust before their eyes. In seconds there was nothing left of him, just a heap of dusty black clothing at their feet.

'Cellular collapse,' said the Doctor softly.

'In all my years as a pathologist I've never seen anything like it,' gasped Litefoot.

'Let's hope you never do again, Professor.'

'But was *was* he?' asked Jago. 'Where was he from?'

The Doctor clapped him on the shoulder. 'A foe from the future, Henry. Let's leave it at that.' Crossing to the Time Cabinet the Doctor closed and locked it —just as a small, malevolent figure leaped from the top of the Dragon idol straight on to Leela's shoulders, a long sharp knife in its hand. Jago and Litefoot ran forward to pull it off. The knife flashed down, and Litefoot staggered back with a cry, blood welling from a wound in his arm. Locking his legs tightly around Leela's neck Mr Sin raised the knife again. The Doctor sprang forward, thrusting Jago out of the way. He wrenched the dummy from Leela's shoulders with one savage heave. Leela staggered back choking, and the Doctor dashed the manikin to the ground with all his strength. He lifted it, slammed it to the floor facedown, groped between, beneath the embroidered tunic and wrenched out a slim metallic tube, flung it to the ground and stamped on it.

'That was what you might call his fuse,' he gasped. 'He's harmless now. As harmless as a ventriloquist's dummy.' The Doctor disentangled the crystal pendant from the pile of black clothes, dropped it beside Sin and ground it to fragments beneath his heel. The

138

anger faded from his face and he smiled wearily at the others. 'There! The Zygma experiment is finally at an end.' He paused. 'Listen!'

They heard a bell ringing in the distance, and a faint muffled cry. 'The muffin man,' said the Doctor happily. 'Come on, I'll treat you all to some muffins!'

They said their farewells over hot tea and buttered muffins in Professor Litefoot's house, then the Doctor insisted politely but firmly that he and Leela must be on their way. He had no wish to become involved in the lengthy investigations that were sure to follow.

Leela was still munching the last of the muffin as they strolled through the night streets back to the TARDIS. Litefoot, his arm in a sling, was doing his best to teach Leela the rudiments of polite behaviour. 'For example, I would say: "One lump or two, Miss Leela?" and you would reply, "One will suffice, thank you."'

'Suppose I want two?'

'No, no, my dear. One lump for ladies.'

'Then why ask me?'

Litefoot scratched his head.

'Do come along, Leela,' called the Doctor. They turned the corner, and there was the TARDIS where they had left it.

'Professor Litefoot has been explaining about tea,' said Leela. 'It is very complicated.'

The Doctor was in a hurry to be off. 'Well, unfortunately we don't have time for any more tea parties. Good-bye, Professor, good-bye, Henry.' He shook hands with them both, unlocked the TARDIS door and ushered Leela inside.

Rather astonished by this abrupt disappearance, Litefoot turned to Jago. 'I though he said he was leaving. What is that contraption?'

Jago hadn't the slightest idea, but was reluctant to admit it. 'Provided by Scotland Yard,' he said vaguely. 'Look, it says "POLICE" on it. Perhaps it's a small portable Police Station!'

There was a wheezing, groaning sound, and the TARDIS faded away before their astonished eyes.

'Extraordinary,' breathed Litefoot. 'I just don't believe it!'

'I've said it before and I'll say it again,' said Jago. 'Our policemen are wonderful.'

As they turned to go, Litefoot was still spluttering, 'But it's impossible. Quite impossible!'

Jago nodded appreciatively. 'Good trick that, eh?' His eye was caught by a poster for his own theatre. Chang's face looked out at him, and Jago reminded himself that he would have to start looking for a new top-of-the-bill act. 'Yes,' said Jago thoughtfully, 'I venture to say that not even the great Li H'sen Chang himself could have pulled off a better trick than that.' He took Litefoot's arm and led him away. 'Now then Professor, I suggest we round off this extraordinary evening with a celebratory libation. It so happens I know a little tavern not too far from here...'

Chang's face stared out from the poster as their footsteps faded away into the fog.

| | | | |
|---|---|---|---|
| 200098 | Terrance Dicks<br>DOCTOR WHO AND THE<br>HORROR OF FANG ROCK | | 60p |
| 108663 | Brian Hayles<br>DOCTOR WHO AND THE ICE WARRIORS | | 60p |
| 110412 | Terrance Dicks<br>DOCTOR WHO AND THE LOCH NESS<br>MONSTER | | 60p |
| 118936 | Philip Hinchcliffe<br>DOCTOR WHO AND THE MASQUE<br>OF MANDRAGORA | | 60p |
| 116909 | Terrance Dicks<br>DOCTOR WHO AND THE MUTANTS | | 60p |
| 116828 | Terrance Dicks<br>DOCTOR WHO AND THE PLANET<br>OF EVIL | | 60p |
| 116666 | Terrance Dicks<br>DOCTOR WHO AND THE PYRAMIDS<br>OF MARS | | 60p |
| 11308X | Malcolm Hulke<br>DOCTOR WHO AND THE<br>SEA-DEVILS | (illus) | 40p |
| 116585 | Philip Hinchcliffe<br>DOCTOR WHO AND THE SEEDS<br>OF DOOM | | 50p |
| 110331 | Malcolm Hulke<br>DOCTOR WHO AND THE SPACE WAR | | 60p |
| 119738 | Terrance Dicks<br>DOCTOR WHO AND THE TALONS OF<br>WENG–CHIANG | | 60p |
| 110846 | Terrance Dicks<br>DOCTOR WHO AND THE WEB OF FEAR | | 60p |
| 113241 | Bill Strutton<br>DOCTOR WHO AND THE ZARBI | (illus) | 60p |
| 114477 | Terrance Dicks<br>THE DOCTOR WHO MONSTER BOOK | (illus) | 50p |
| 200012 | THE SECOND DOCTOR WHO<br>MONSTER BOOK | (Colour illus ) | 70p |
| 118421 | Terrance Dicks<br>THE DOCTOR WHO DINOSAUR BOOK | | 75p |
| 116151 | Terrance Dicks and Malcolm Hulke<br>THE MAKING OF DOCTOR WHO | | 60p |

†For sale in Britain and Ireland only.
*Not for sale in Canada.
♦ Film & T.V. tie-ins.

# TARGET STORY BOOKS

## 'Doctor Who'

| | | | | | |
|---|---|---|---|---|---|
| 200020 | DOCTOR WHO DISCOVERS PREHISTORIC ANIMALS | (NF) | (illus) | 75p |
| 200039 | DOCTOR WHO DISCOVERS SPACE TRAVEL | (NF) | (illus) | 75p |
| 200047 | DOCTOR WHO DISCOVERS STRANGE AND MYSTERIOUS CREATURES | (NF) | (illus) | 75p |
| 20008X | DOCTOR WHO DISCOVERS THE STORY OF EARLY MAN | (NF) | (illus) | 75p |
| 200136 | DOCTOR WHO DISCOVERS THE CONQUERORS | (NF) | (illus) | 75p |

Ian Marter
116313 DOCTOR WHO AND THE ARK IN SPACE     50p

Terrance Dicks
116747 DOCTOR WHO AND THE BRAIN OF MORBIUS     50p*

Terrance Dicks
110250 DOCTOR WHO AND THE CARNIVAL
OF MONSTERS     50p

Malcolm Hulke
11471X DOCTOR WHO AND THE CAVE
MONSTERS     60p

Terrance Dicks
117034 DOCTOR WHO AND THE CLAWS
OF AXOS     50p*

David Whitaker
113160 DOCTOR WHO AND THE CRUSADERS     (illus)   60p

Brian Hayles
114981 DOCTOR WHO AND THE CURSE
OF PELADON     60p

Gerry Davis
114639 DOCTOR WHO AND THE CYBERMEN     60p

Barry Letts
113322 DOCTOR WHO AND THE DAEMONS     (illus)   40p

David Whitaker
101103 DOCTOR WHO AND THE DALEKS     60p

Terrance Dicks
11244X DOCTOR WHO AND THE DALEK
INVASION OF EARTH     60p

Terrance Dicks
119657 DOCTOR WHO AND THE DEADLY ASSASSIN     60p

Terrance Dicks
200063 DOCTOR WHO AND THE FACE
OF EVIL     60p

Terrance Dicks
112601 DOCTOR WHO AND THE GENESIS
OF THE DALEKS     60p

†For sale in Britain and Ireland only.
*Not for sale in Canada.
♦ Film & T.V. tie-ins.

# TARGET STORY BOOKS

## Fantasy And General Fiction

| | | | |
|---|---|---|---|
| | Elisabeth Beresford | | |
| 101537 | **AWKWARD MAGIC** | (illus) | 60p |
| 10479X | **SEA-GREEN MAGIC** | (illus) | 60p |
| 101618 | **TRAVELLING MAGIC** | (illus) | 60p |
| | Eileen Dunlop | | |
| 119142 | **ROBINSHEUGH** | (illus) | 60p |
| | Maria Gripe | | |
| 112288 | **THE GLASSBLOWER'S CHILDREN** | (illus) | 45p |
| | Joyce Nicholson | | |
| 117891 | **FREEDOM FOR PRISCILLA** | | 70p |
| | Hilary Seton | | |
| 106989 | **THE HUMBLES** | (illus) | 50p |
| 109112 | **THE NOEL STREATFEILD CHRISTMAS HOLIDAY BOOK** | (illus) | 60p |
| 109031 | **THE NOEL STREATFEILD EASTER HOLIDAY BOOK** | (illus) | 60p |
| 105249 | **THE NOEL STREATFEILD SUMMER HOLIDAY BOOK** | (illus) | 50p |

## Humour

| | | | |
|---|---|---|---|
| | Eleanor Estes | | |
| 107519 | **THE WITCH FAMILY** | (illus) | 50p |
| | Felice Holman | | |
| 11762X | **THE WITCH ON THE CORNER** | (illus) | 50p |
| | Spike Milligan | | |
| 105672 | **BADJELLY THE WITCH** | (illus) | 60p |
| 109546 | **DIP THE PUPPY** | (illus) | 60p |
| | Christine Nostlinger | | |
| 107438 | **THE CUCUMBER KING** | (illus) | 45p |
| | Mary Rogers | | |
| 119223 | **A BILLION FOR BORIS** | | 60p |

## 0426    Film And TV Tie-ins

| | | | |
|---|---|---|---|
| | Kathleen N. Daly | | |
| 200187 | **RAGGEDY ANN AND ANDY** (Colour illus) | 75p | ♦ * |
| | John Ryder Hall | | |
| 11826X | **SINBAD AND THE EYE OF THE TIGER** | 70p* | ♦ |
| | John Lucarotti | | |
| 11535X | **OPERATION PATCH** | 45p | |
| | Pat Sandys | | |
| 119495 | **THE PAPER LADS** | 60p | ♦ |
| | Alison Thomas | | |
| 115511 | **BENJI** | 40p | |

†For sale in Britain and Ireland only.
*Not for sale in Canada.
♦ Film & T.V. tie-ins.

Wyndham Books are obtainable from many booksellers and newsagents. If you have any difficulty please send purchase price plus postage on the scale below to:

**Wyndham Cash Sales**
**P.O. Box 11**
**Falmouth**
**Cornwall**

While every effort is made to keep prices low, it is sometimes necessary to increase prices at short notice. Wyndham Books reserve the right to show new retail prices on covers which may differ from those advertised in the text or elsewhere.

**Postage and Packing Rate**

**UK:** 22p for the first book, plus 10p per copy for each additional book ordered to a maximum charge of 82p. **BFPO and Eire:** 22p for the first book, plus 10p per copy for the next 6 books and thereafter 4p per book. **Overseas:** 30p for the first book and 10p per copy for each additional book.

These charges are subject to Post Office charge fluctuations.